Short Stories Two

Compiled by Roger Mansfield

Illustrated by Neville Swaine,

SCHOFIELD & SIMS LTD., HUDDERSFIELD

0 7217 0301 1
0 7217 0331 3 Net edition

First printed 1977
Reprinted 1978
Reprinted 1981

發行人：周　　　　　　政
發行所：敦煌書局股份有限公司
地　址：台北市中山北路2段103號
電　話：(02) 537·1666（總機）
郵　撥：0 0 1 4 1 0 3 — 1
印刷所：聯和印製廠有限公司
新聞局登記證局版台業字0269號
中華民國74年 9月　　　日第　版

CONTENTS

ACKNOWLEDGEMENTS

The compiler and publishers wish to thank the following for permission to use copyright material:

Rosemary Sutcliff, for 'The Bridge-Builders' from 'Another Six' published by Basil Blackwell.

William Mayne and Faber and Faber Ltd., for 'A Prince in the Building' by William Mayne from 'Over the Horizon or Around the World in 15 Stories' published by Victor Gollancz.

John Wyndham and Michael Joseph Ltd., for 'Meteor' by John Wyndham from 'The Seeds of Time'.

Eilís Dillon and Faber and Faber Ltd., for 'Bad Blood' by Eilís Dillon from 'The Faber Book of Stories'.

Mrs. Helen Thurber, for Canadian rights in 'The Secret Life of Walter Mitty' © 1942 James Thurber. © 1970 Helen Thurber. From 'My World – and Welcome to it', published by Harcourt Brace Jovanovich, New York. Originally printed in 'The New Yorker'. Hamish Hamilton Ltd., for British Commonwealth rights in 'The Secret Life of Walter Mitty' from 'Vintage Thurber' Volume 1. The Collection Copyright © 1963 Hamish Hamilton, London.

René Guillot and George G. Harrap and Co. Ltd., for 'The Lion Cubs' from 'Beyond the Bambassu' by René Guillot.

Alan Garner and Macmillan Publishers Ltd., for 'Galgoid the Hewer' by Alan Garner from 'Winter's Tales for Children'.

The Estate of the late H. E. Bates and Jonathan Cape Ltd., for 'Silas the Good' from 'My Uncle Silas' by H. Bates.

INTRODUCTION

The line between stories for adults and stories for children is an imprecise one. Some critics and writers have even suggested that no distinction can be drawn between the two. In terms of intrinsic literary quality, this argument certainly holds true. There is no reason why lower standards should apply to literature intended for children; no reason why younger readers should be satisfied with hackneyed plots, stereotyped characters, unconvincing action or trivial themes. There are, however, other considerations. Any reader must be able to respond to a book.

> One does not write *for* children. One writes so that children can understand. Which means writing as clearly, vividly and truthfully as possible.
>
> Leon Garfield

If a story goes too far beyond a reader's experience or imagination, or if the style and vocabulary present tedious barriers, there will be no communication. And if this happens too often, there is a real possibility that reading, as an enjoyable and worthwhile recreation, will be discarded. It is on these grounds that teachers, librarians and parents are justified in distinguishing between literature for children and books for adults. But to exaggerate the gap can be as dangerous as to ignore it.

> One does indeed write *for* children, but there isn't really any Great Divide.
>
> John Rowe Townsend

The aim of this series is to reduce the risk that younger readers themselves will see a Great Divide where none exists, to present stories that are both accessible and, at the same time, capable of widening horizons—stories that the reader will *always* enjoy, whatever his or her age.

> A children's story which is enjoyed only by children is a bad children's book.
>
> C. S. Lewis

Rosemary Sutcliff

Rosemary Sutcliff was born in 1920. Her father was a naval officer and, until he retired, she and her mother accompanied him on his travels from one dockyard to another. Since she was two years old, she has suffered from a polyarthritic complaint which has restricted her physical movement. As a result, she did not begin proper schooling until she was nine. Before that her mother taught her and also read her many stories, which paved the way for her own writing.

"When I was six or seven years old, my mother first read me *A Centurion of the Thirtieth* and then the two other stories about Roman Britain in Kipling's *Puck of Pook's Hill*. I loved these stories and Roman Britain has fascinated me ever since. And so when I came to write stories of my own, after a while I found that I, too, wanted to write stories about Roman Britain."

Her books about this period include: *The Eagle of the Ninth* and *The Silver Branch*, both dealing with the lost standard of the Ninth Legion; *Outcast*, about a galley slave; *The Lantern Bearers*, set at the time when the Legions were being withdrawn from Britain and Saxon invaders were pouring in; and *The Mark of the Horse Lord*, telling of a Roman gladiator. THE BRIDGE-BUILDERS is about life in a Roman frontier fort.

Rosemary Sutcliff left school when she was fourteen to train as a painter. She became an expert professional miniaturist but in her mid-twenties gave up painting to concentrate on writing. She lives in a country cottage near Arundel in Sussex, "just half the county away from where *Puck of Pook's Hill* was written".

The Bridge-Builders

by Rosemary Sutcliff

Androphon squatted on the skin rug, playing with Math, his father's great Hibernian wolf-hound, and listening with one ear to his father and mother talking, and with the other to the evening life of the frontier fort going on outside, and the silence of the mountains outside again. All his twelve years, until a few months ago, he had lived quietly with his mother at Durinum, while his father soldiered up and down Britain; or in the town outside the fortress walls of Deva, where all the garrison wives and families lived. And it still seemed to him strange and exciting to be right up here into the western mountains, in a frontier fort more than a day's march from the next Roman station.

Outside in the twilight that was water green beyond the window of the Commander's quarters, a trumpet sang; someone went marching by along the colonnade, studded sandals ringing on the pavement, and stretching his ears, Androphon heard a sharp challenge and reply, and the clash of a grounded pilum. That would be the Duty Centurion doing First Rounds.

"He sat there with his bodyguard leaning on their spears behind him," Androphon's father was saying, "and said to me: 'Rome has come far enough into these mountains. Let the Commander forget the matter of this signal tower, and we also will forget, and there will be no harm done.' "

"And what did you say?" asked Androphon's mother, and let the tunic that she was mending fall into her lap.

"I said: 'O Kyndylan the Chieftain, lord of five hundred spears. I am not my own master, to remember or forget at my own will.

Caesar, whom I serve, bids me to build a signal tower on the hill shoulder above the Pass of the Wild Cat, that the talking beacon may carry as far as Canovium, as it could not do if we built it here, because of the mountains in between. And as Caesar orders, so I build.' And he sat there and hooded his eyes a little (he has yellow eyes, like a wolf's) and said: 'Then my young men will make trouble.' Meaning that *he* would. I said to him: 'It would be wiser that your young men do not make trouble; Rome is strong, even here in the mountains.' And he said: 'But then the young are seldom wise.' "

Androphon held Math's rough head and looked into his eyes—they were yellow, too; he came of a breed that had hunted men before now—and went on listening.

"And what now?" his mother asked quietly.

"We shall start building operations tomorrow."

"And there will be trouble?"

"Oh, yes. Not bad trouble, I think, not the sort that ends up in a punitive expedition and a village burned; but trouble, none the less. Stone will be difficult to get, and the transport ponies will go sick, and there'll be a few fatal accidents. And it is all so needless——" Suddenly the Commander crashed up from his camp chair and began to stride about the small lamplit room. "It is all so needless, if only one could find the right way—find the meeting-point; British and Roman, we can speak the same language in words, oh yes, but words are not enough. . . . Sometimes, Claudia, I feel as though we were shouting at each other across a river, just too wide for either of us to hear what the other says. We need some kind of bridge. . . ."

Androphon looked up, and saw that his father's black brows had drawn almost to meeting point across the top of his big nose; and Math whimpered softly, then got up and padded to and fro beside him.

"No, I don't believe that there will be bad trouble," the Commander said after a little. "But all the same, I am giving orders that no one is to leave the camp for the present, though I shall not interfere with the native traders coming in." He stopped in his tracks, looking down at the boy. "That order is for you, also—and for Math."

"Math won't like it," Androphon said, scrambling to his feet. "He likes hunting hares; we both do."

"The hares will wait," said his father. "You understand, Androphon?"

He said it as though he were on the parade ground, and as though he were on the parade ground, Androphon jumped slightly, and snapped to attention. "I understand, Father."

The lower camp was outside the fort, but joined on to it. The bath-house was there, and the wine shop and the women's quarters; and there the traders came and went with skins and hunting dogs and cooking pots to sell to the garrison and their wives; and often you might watch a cockfight, or a magic-maker from the hills, half-mad, who could make a knife drip blood of its own accord or a pebble turn to a blue flower in his hand, if you gave him a denarius. Androphon spent a good deal of time in the lower camp, watching things and poking about and picking up the language; for these mountain men spoke a tongue that was different in some ways from the tongue of the Lowland British that he had spoken all his life as easily as he did Latin.

Late on the third day after building started on the new signal tower (they had already had an unexplained stampede of ponies in the middle of the night, and a man almost killed by a block of stone that mysteriously slipped), Androphon and Math were on their way back from the farthest corner of the camp, because their stomachs as well as the westering light told them that it was supper time. The camp was swarming with things to look at as usual; and the boy and the dog did not hurry themselves, but stopped to look at this and that by the way, until they came up by the gateway in the turf wall that led out towards the mountains; and there they stopped again, to watch a trader who had come in earlier that day with beaver skins and silver ornaments, setting off on his homeward way.

And it was not until the trader was finally gone into the long evening shadows that Androphon found that Math was gone, too.

At first he thought that the great hound had only wandered off into the coming and going of the camp, and he whistled and called, "Math! Ma-ath!" but no Math came; and in a little he realised with sharp anxiety that he must have slipped out after the trader, or following some hunting smell that had come to him on the wind.

And what must he do now? Father had said that no one was to leave the camp. "That order is for you also," he had said, "and for Math." And now Math was out somewhere, running free in the mountains that had grown hostile in the last three days, and the shadows were lengthening and soon it would be dusk. . . . Androphon stood for a few moments, thinking; then he glanced round to see if anyone was watching him. No one; he was quite alone.

With his heart suddenly hammering against his ribs, because he had never disobeyed his father before, he slipped out and ran.

From the bend of the track he could see the trader and his pony dwindling down the valley; but of Math, no sign. Maybe he had gone upward. Androphon and he had hunted on the higher skirts

10

of the mountain more than once before the trouble started, and maybe he would remember. The boy turned his face to the slopes that rose above him through midge-infested woods of hazel and hawthorn to the bare mountain flanks above that seemed growing in menace as the daylight faded, and began to climb.

How long he searched, whistling and calling, looking every moment for the brindled shape of the great hound leaping towards him through the dusk—looking also, with his blood jumping uncomfortably, for lurking tribesmen behind every bush—he never knew. Math, bored with three days within walls, was off on some hunting trail of his own, and never even heard the whistling and calling that died away behind him into the wind-haunted silence of the great hills. It was quite dark, though the first snail-silver of the rising moon was spreading above the mountains eastward, when his searching ended; and it ended, not because he found Math, but because between one step and the next, the ground went from under him and he pitched forward and down with a yell and a scrabble of falling stones, the whole night turned over and over about him, and something burst like a bright flower of flame in his left temple, and he shot out into roaring blackness.

The next thing he knew was the full moon just breaking clear of the mountain shoulder; and he was lying on his back on the soft springiness of young heather, at the foot of a sheer scarp of rock. Then a voice spoke quite close by, and another answered, and he realised with a stab of terror, through the throbbing and swimming of his head, that three men were standing around him. And they were not men from the fort.

He scrambled to his elbow, the world spinning and swooping around him, and fumbled wildly for the knife in his belt; the little slim hunting knife that his father had given him. One of the men caught it from him. "Ah, now! What a little fighting cock! Maybe he'll have his value if we take him back to the village."

Androphon understood them well enough, and, too dizzy and terrified to know fully what he did, cried out furiously: "You let me alone! My father is the Commander of the fort down yonder, and if you do not let me go, he'll—he'll burn your houses down and salt your fields!"

There was a little silence after he had said it; only a late curlew calling somewhere over the heather; and the men looked at each other, and suddenly he saw that they were laughing, as though at some jest that he did not understand—almost silent laughter that made dark streaks in their faces in the moonlight.

"So-o, here is a most fortunate thing; it seems that our hunting has been better than we thought," said the man who sounded to be their leader; and then: "Load him on to the spare pony, my brothers—and let you be careful how you handle him; it is in my mind that he is of more use to us living than dead."

Androphon, as the world began to steady, saw that the men had hounds with them, and two ponies, one loaded down with the great limp carcass of a deer, the other unburdened. He began to struggle and shout as he felt their hands on him. "Let me go! Let me go!" But even if he had not been half-stunned, he was only one twelve-year-old boy in the grip of three grown men. With contemptuous ease that took no account of his kicking and biting, they loaded him on to the spare pony, and tied his ankles with a hide rope under its belly, and with the world swimming more wildly than ever, he sagged forward on to the pony's neck, as they began to urge it forward.

He saw nothing of the way they went, the two ponies with their live and dead loads, and the hounds and men loping alongside. He saw the moon-brushed darkness of the heather sliding and swaying and heaving past beneath the ponies' hooves, and he thought that the ground was nearly always rising; and it seemed a very long way.

The moon was swimming clear and high when the hunting party came to a halt at last; and he was confusedly aware of movement all about him, people pulling away something like a thorn bush from the gate-gap in a bank and stockade, voices that questioned and answered and exclaimed, and laughed that same quiet laughter as at a jest that he did not understand. The ponies were moving on again through the gap, and when they stopped for good, he had a vague idea that they were in a village; the smell of peat smoke and horse droppings and garbage was on the air, and a torch was flaring somewhere. A man untied his ankles, and caught him as he slid from the pony's back, and, carrying him in through a house-place doorway, flung him down beside a fire that had been smothered for the night and showed only a few red embers glowing in the darkness.

There were people all round him. Someone was waking the fire, breaking up the black mass and throwing on birch logs and peat; and somebody—he thought it was a woman—gave him a bowl of clear mountain water to drink; and he gulped and gulped, and a good deal of it ran down his chin, but the world began to steady from that moment; and in a little while he got his head up and began to see what lay around him.

He was in a long place like a barn, with the fire burning on a raised hearth in the centre, and the red light of the flames that were now waking and leaping up towards the rafters, beat upon the fierce, bright-eyed faces of the men crowding close around it; on the checkered garments that they wore; on the brindled hide of a hound; here and there on an ornament of gold or silver or bronze. Androphon saw that one of the men wore the golden torc of a chieftain round his neck, and his eyes were wolf yellow; and as soon as he spoke, he knew him for the same man who had seemed to be the leader of the hunting party.

"It is in my heart that we will let the thing lie for one day," the

Chieftain was saying reflectively. "One day for the Commander's fears to ripen; then I will go down to him and say again, 'Let us forget this matter of the signal tower!' "

Androphon did not quite know how he got there, but he found himself on his feet, facing the Chieftain as proudly and furiously as he could, though the ferny floor still rocked beneath him. "He will not listen to you!" he shouted. "He will not listen to you, what*ever* you say!"

The Chieftain's yellow eyes seemed to hood themselves a little. "Not though I say to him that his son lies within my walls?"

And then Androphon knew what the jest had been that he did not understand.

He cried out in wild defiance: "I shall not be long within your walls! My father will find me and—and burn your hall down and *still* build the signal station! Very soon, my father will come—maybe he's on the way now!"

"So? And has the Commander, then, the nose of a hound, to follow your track all this way?" said the Chieftain, settling himself comfortably on his skin-spread stool beside the hearth; and the silent laughter that had made dark streaks in his face in the moonlight made them now in the light of the fire.

"He will know that you have me in your village, and he'll catch a hunter and make him tell where it is."

"Aiee! but then you will not be in my village, little fighting cock. Tomorrow you will go to a safe hiding-place farther into the mountains, and it is in my mind that the Commander will not catch an eagle to tell him where *that* is."

Fear was rising in Androphon's throat, but he fought it back and shut his teeth on it. "You will be sorry," he said in a choking voice. "Remember, my father told you that Rome is strong, even in the mountains!"

The Chieftain had been playing with a knife—Androphon's own little hunting knife—as he talked, weighing it from hand to hand. Suddenly he leaned forward, laughing still, and touched the point of it to the boy's throat low down, just between the collar bones. And as Androphon tried to step back, he felt other points pricking him from behind and on either flank, and caught all round him the glint and gleam of bare blades in the firelight, the

14

flash of eyes and the whiteness of teeth between back-turned, grinning lips. "You see? I have but to drive this in a little, where it only kisses now, and roll what is left of the Commander's son into the nearest bog, and who is to know any more, until night and day become one, than that he got lost in the mountains and was no more seen. Poor child, doubtless it was the wolves." Kyndylan the Chieftain pressed the dagger very delicately into the brown skin at the base of Androphon's neck, just enough to feel like a horsefly's sting, no more. "You see, little fighting cock? What can your Rome do for you now?"

Androphon shut his teeth tighter and tighter. He was desperately afraid; he had not known before that anyone could be so afraid without crumbling away altogether. And yet nothing seemed real; it was like a dream—one of the dark dreams from which one wakes up sweating and screaming.

And then a boy's voice from the outskirts of the group said with cool interest: "What is it that you do here?"

The Chieftain withdrew the knife a finger's breadth, and glanced up, most of the other men doing the same; and with a shuddering gasp, Androphon craned his head round also. He saw a boy of about his own age or maybe a few months older; a very tall boy, with red hair that curled in rings about his ears and neck, and big bones that stood out under his skin, and a look about him as though maybe the firelight might shine right through him and come out the other side.

"We make a little sport," said the Chieftain, speaking as man to man. "What is it that *you* do here, Cador, my son?" And he let his hand with the dagger sink back on to his knee.

"The voices and firelight woke me, O Kyndylan, my father," said the boy; but he was staring at Androphon. "Is that what you brought back from your hunting?"

"A buck as well; but this that is of more value than many bucks, for it is the son of the fort Commander down yonder."

The boy looked Androphon up and down, and whistled very softly between his teeth, "Aiee! What is it that you will do with him?"

"Bargain a little with the Commander, in the matter of a certain signal tower."

"Meanwhile, I will take him."

He said it as he might have done if he were speaking of a hound puppy; and Androphon felt the hairs rising on the back of his neck as though he had been a hound puppy indeed. The men laughed, and Kyndylan said: "And why will you take him?"

"Because I want him. I never saw a Roman boy before. I thought they were all a dark people, but he is nearly as red as I am. He shall sleep under my rug tonight."

"Shall he so? And are you, then, already the Chieftain, to say 'this shall be' and 'that shall not be'?" Kyndylan said, but as though he was fiercely pleased, rather than angry. And he tossed the hunting knife to Cador, who caught it as it spun, grinning. "Let you take him, then, and take also his knife in token that he is yours until I claim him of you."

Cador stood with the knife in his hand, and looked at Androphon; and Androphon, turned full towards him now, looked back, while the men watched; and for no very clear reason, the hairs on the back of the Roman boy's neck laid themselves down again. Then, with a backward jerk of his head, Cador said: "Come away." And on legs that did not feel like his own, Androphon found himself stumbling after him.

Cador led the way to the far end of the hall, where the firelight scarcely reached, and stopped at one of the narrow sleeping stalls that lined the wall there. "Let you get in and lie down," he said, reaching up to put the hunting knife in a niche in the wall above. And Androphon, as much because his legs were giving way beneath him and his head swimming in a kind of fiery fog as for any other reason, plunged forward into the warm darkness that might have been an animal's lair, and had, a little, the same feeling of refuge.

He felt the springy softness of piled fern beneath him, and he pressed back against the wall and lay rigid, while the other boy crawled in beside him. Cador dragged up the tumbled sleeping-rug that felt like deerskins, and flung it over both of them, heads and all; and the firelight was shut out, and the voices of the men grew muffled and far off. And in the warm, animal-smelling darkness, he put up a hand and felt the broken place on Androphon's temple with a kind of rough friendliness.

"Did they do that?"

"No, I fell down some rocks—it was so that they found me."

"What is your name?"

"Androphon."

"An-dro-phon. Mine is Cador. You know my tongue?"

"I have not lived all my life in Britain with my ears shut like an oyster. It is different, here in the mountains, but I understand, mostly." Androphon caught a furious breath. "I understand enough to know that your father means to use me for a—a hostage against the signal tower."

"That is between your father and mine, not between you and me," said the British boy. "Even if they kill you, it is still not between you and me. But they shall not kill you if I can help it."

The two boys lay on the southward slope of the chariot shed roof, flat out and basking like a couple of hounds in the sunshine that was hot already, though the sun had not long shaken clear of

the mountains. Below them, the life of the village went on among
the crowding turf- and bracken-thatched huts, and dropping away
beyond the stockade, the heather and bilberry already shimmered
in the young summer heat. The turf of the roof under them was
warm and live as a hound's coat, and the little rowan tree that had
rooted itself there, though it stood only half as tall as a man, was
curdled with creamy blossom, and the honey scent of it laced the

air all about them, mingled with the blue waft of peat smoke from the houseplace fires; and Androphon was more sharply aware of all these things than he had ever been of anything before. He had stopped being afraid; it was as though he had come through to the other side of fear. He was just living every moment as it came; and oddly, the present moment had a sort of goodness to it. Soon, even between this breath and the next, they might come to drag him off through the heather to the hidden place that Kyndylan had spoken of. But meanwhile, his head no longer ached and they had given him barley bannock and honey, as much as he could eat, at the morning meal; there was an amber bee droning among the rowan flowers, and an eagle circling and circling the blue air high overhead. He turned on to his elbow, to look at Cador, who lay on his back with his arms and legs flung wide; Cador wearing two knives in the belt about his narrow waist, his own which had coral studs in the hilt, and the little slim hunting knife that was really Androphon's; and suddenly he asked a thing that he had been wondering for some time. "Why does your father let you do just as you please about all things? I don't believe my father would let me take a captive of his away for myself, just because I had a mind to."

Cador grinned, watching the eagle as it came round in another great curve, tipping its wings to the wind currents of the upper air. "That is because I have been ill. I was so ill that he thought I should go beyond the sunset, and he would have no son to be Chieftain after him. Now I am well again, and presently, when he has forgotten a little, he will not let me do as I please any more; but meanwhile—it is good."

There was a little silence, and then Androphon said very carefully, stroking the warm turf as he spoke: "Cador, if you begged your father to let me go—he would not do that for you, would he?"

Cador brought his gaze down from the circling eagle, and turned his head on the turf to look at Androphon. "No," he said after a few moments. "He would not do that for me. You know too much, Androphon; you know where the village is, and about his plans to use you as a hostage. There is too much that you could tell."

Androphon looked at his brown hand spread-fingered on the

tawny turf. Then he looked again at the British boy. "Cador, if you were my father's hostage, and I helped you to escape, and you knew that there was a—a weak spot in the fortress walls, would you tell?"

"I don't know," Cador said, frowningly; and then, after a little silence, "If I were to help you to escape, would *you* tell?"

"I don't know, either."

They stared at each other in silence, both frowning now, puzzled and somehow wary, caught up in a queer mingling of feelings that pulled them two ways at once and hurt them in places where they had never been hurt before.

And in the silence, from the hill shoulder away south-eastward, came the note of a horn, small and clear on the sunny hill air. And before the echoes died, from somewhere farther off still, a hound bayed twice and was silent.

The two boys had started into a sitting position, facing each other as though frozen. "That is the watcher of our ways. Someone is coming up the valley," Cador said.

And Androphon cried out in a kind of cracked, exultant whisper: "That is Math, my father's hound! Your father said he hadn't a hound's nose to follow me all this way, but——"

Cador's eyes were darkly blazing in a face that had turned a queer pearly colour. "You must hide. Come——"

"Hide? I'll not hide! Why should I?"

"*Come*! Don't you see? My father will do *anything* to keep you from being found here. You must hide until your father is within the gates, then you'll be safe."

He had rolled over on to his belly, and was off like a lizard round the curve of the roof, looking back once to make sure that Androphon was coming. And without question, almost without thought, where clearly there was no time for thought or questioning, Androphon darted after him. Other smaller sheds and barns and byres crowded in the rear of the great chariot shed, and with the village already rousing into purposeful activity behind them, first Cador and then Androphon dropped from the roof—it was little more than breast high at the back—and ran for the shelter of the nearest byre. There they checked a moment, their hearts pounding, their ears on the stretch for any sound that would tell them they had been sighted. But there was none. "This way," Cador whispered. "Quick!" and they darted on again.

Following hard on Cador's heels, Androphon rounded the back of a long brushwood pile, dived under a couple of the little raised sheds where the seed corn was stored, and at last plunged in through the dark entrance of a byre. They were greeted by a gigantic stirring in the umber shadows, and a great puff of breath as a huge red beast lifted its head to watch them, pawing at the ground. "It is naught to fear," Cador said. "It is Belu, my father's herd bull, but he knows me. Hai! Belu! Up here, on to the fodder rack. Now—up again."

And a few moments later Androphon, gasping for breath, found himself sprawled in the hayloft in the crown of the roof, among the dried clover-grass that was piled there, with Cador, gasping also, whispering to him to get back from the edge and pull some of the hay over his head.

It was not really a good hiding-place; sooner or later it was bound to be searched; but they only needed it to gain them a little time, just enough for the Roman troops to reach the village. "They'll search the chariot shed first, because the last time anyone saw us we were on the roof," Cador muttered, as though he knew what Androphon was thinking. "And if anyone but my father comes in here, they'll have trouble with Belu, and that will take time, too." And after that neither of them spoke or moved, scarcely breathed, for what seemed a very long while.

They had quite forgotten the moment on the chariot shed roof, their queer feeling of being pulled two ways at once. All that had gone the moment the horn sounded, and they did not even notice, either of them, what a strange thing it was that Cador was doing.

Outside there were voices, the soft pad of running feet in rawhide shoes that seemed to come from all quarters at once; someone calling Cador by name. Inside the byre, it seemed very quiet. They could hear the racing beat of their own hearts and Belu's long puffing breaths; and peering down through a knot hole in the floor of the loft, Androphon could see a bar of sunlight lying like burnished copper across the brute's great red flank. Then gradually another sound rose in the world outside: the soft rolling beat of many horses' hooves. A few moments more, and the hard bright notes of a Roman trumpet were flinging to and fro between the echoing mountains.

Something that was almost a sob rushed up into Androphon's throat. But he did not move. It was Cador who moved, in the moment's breath-held silence that followed, turning towards him in the piled clover-grass with scarcely a rustle. "Here—we may have no chance later—let you take this."

Androphon felt something pressed into his hand, and his fingers closed over the haft of a dagger with little studs in it. "This is not my knife," he whispered.

"No, it is mine."

After that everything seemed to happen very quickly. The trumpet sang again, and the sound of hooves was swelling up between the huts, trampling to a halt, and in the sudden stillness of the halt, Androphon heard, with a gasping relief, a burst of clear-clipped orders in a voice that he knew was his father's.

Cador's legs were already over the edge of the loft. "They will be before my father's hall. Come now," and he dropped. Once again Androphon was close behind him; and once out of Belu's stable, they ran, twisting and swerving like hares among the crowding huts, towards the sounds of Rome.

When they reached the open space before the Chieftain's hall it was full of Roman cavalry; iron-capped and leather-tunicd, sitting their horses in the sunlight, among the watching tribesmen. And before the skin-hung entrance of the hall, Androphon saw his father and Kyndylan standing face to face, the Chieftain leaning on his spear, very perfectly at ease, with his bodyguard behind him, just as though the game that he was playing had not gone amiss, just as though he did not know that his hostage was still at large somewhere in the village and might appear at any moment; and the Commander quietly formidable, with the sun jinking on the hooped bronze shoulder-pieces of his cuirass, and his face very stern in the shadow of his crimson-crested helmet; and the great hound Math sitting against his knee.

"Where is my son?" the Commander was saying, in the voice of one who has asked the question before and means to have an answer.

"Have I not told the Commander that I have not seen his son?"

22

said Kyndylan, in the patient tone of one who had answered the same question more than once.

And even as he spoke, Math raised his head and saw the boy who had checked for an instant on the edge of the open space, and sprang up with a great joyful baying, and came in three long bounds, skiddering among the horses' legs, to fling himself upon him. And next moment, Androphon, sent half-flying, had both arms round the dog's neck and was laughing and almost crying at the same time, while Math licked his face from ear to ear. So he missed all the storm-burst effect of his sudden appearance. But when Math had subsided, and he had got his breath back again, he felt the crackling tension, the brittle, ominous quiet all around him. He saw that his father and Kyndylan had swung around and stood waiting for him; and about them, too, there was that queer, tight quietness. He walked forward again, with his hand on Math's collar, and Cador walking at his shoulder.

"Here I am, Father," he said, and wondered why his mouth felt so uncomfortably dry.

His father looked down at him. "So I see," he said conversationally, and then to Kyndylan: "Why did you tell me that he was not here?"

Kyndylan leaned on his spear and smiled, a small sleepy smile. "Alas! I have always been fond of a jest—maybe too much so."

"There are some things about which it is not wise to jest," said the Commander. He put out a finger and touched the broken place on Androphon's temple. "They did that to you?"

"No." The boy shook his head. "I fell down some rocks while I was looking for Math—he ran away, and that was why I disobeyed you. I had to. How did you—was it Math who found me, Father?"

His father's face had lost none of its sternness. "We turned the whole fort and the lower camp inside out for you; and when Math came back alone, we knew that you had gone beyond the gates. We put Math on to your scent, and he brought us to a place where there was blood on the ground and the traces of ponies. Then we went back and brought out half the garrison in case of trouble, and set Math on to follow the ponies as he had followed you. And since the garrisons of Rome's frontiers have other things to do than hunt disobedient children through the heather, that is a thing about which we will have a reckoning later."

Androphon knew that his father was not as angry as he sounded. He knew that there would indeed be a reckoning later, but he did not think that it would be a very hard one; and, anyway, that was not what mattered. He looked at Kyndylan, and saw the proud and mocking smile in his yellow eyes as he waited for—whatever was coming; and he felt Cador standing rigidly at his shoulder, not knowing whether in saving his friend he had betrayed his people. "Yes, Father," he said, slowly and deliberately, "and—and all the while, I was here. If you had not come so soon, Kyndylan the Chieftain was going to—to send me back to you, before evening." He heard the words as though somebody else was speaking them; and he was aware of a faint movement that was like a breath released from the tribesmen behind Kyndylan; from Kyndylan, no movement at all.

"The sun is well up. Surely it is strange that you had not yet set out," said the Commander.

"It is a holy day of the tribe," murmured Kyndylan in his dark, soft, leaping voice. "I could not let the boy go alone, and on this day of the year it is forbidden to go three bowshots beyond the village until the sun stands over the mountain-crest yonder."

The Commander's mouth twitched a little at the corners, as though he also could appreciate a jest; but his eyes were grave on Androphon's face. "They have been good to you, then? You are sure?"

Androphon stood up very straight before him; and he thought about last night's daggers in the firelight. "Yes," he said.

His father put a hand on his shoulder, and went on searching deep into his face. Then he turned his head abruptly to Kyndylan. "So — I thank you for your care of the boy. For *that*, peace be to you, and good hunting." And his hand still on his son's shoulder, he swung round to call up the soldier who stood by holding his horse.

He was already reaching out to take the reins, with a quick "You will ride on my saddle-bow, Androphon." But Androphon, his heart suddenly beating hard and urgent again, stood immovable before him, his head up, and his hand on the unfamiliar dagger with the coral studs in his belt.

He said in his very best British, looking from one to the other of the two men: "O my Father and Kyndylan the Chieftain, I wish for leave to come again among these hills—often; for Cador and I have exchanged weapons, and henceforward we hunt together."

The Commander let his hand fall slowly on to his horse's neck, and looked down at the two boys, one after the other. Then, but as though he were deeply sorry, he shook his head. "The order still stands, my son. There is still the matter of the signal station, remember." He turned again to Kyndylan, as though in courteous explanation. "We have been having certain troubles in the building of a certain signal tower; maybe you have heard? And while the trouble lasts, I have given orders—you see how well they are obeyed—that no one goes outside the camp without my leave."

Kyndylan returned his look as straightly as it was given; and for a long, long moment there was no sound save for the fidgeting among the horses and the sharp cry of the circling eagle pricking the silence of the high hills; then his yellow eyes went to the two boys; to his own son, and to Androphon, and back again to the Commander.

"I had heard. It is in my mind that in the building of this new signal tower there will be no more trouble," said Kyndylan the Chieftain.

William Mayne

William Mayne was born in 1928, the eldest of five children of a doctor and a nurse. He was educated at the Canterbury Cathedral Choir School, which provided the setting for his third novel, *A Swarm in May*, the book that established him as a leading author for young people. It tells the story of John Owen, the youngest chorister at the school, who refuses to carry on tradition by acting as the cathedral's beekeeper, thinking he dislikes bees. But in helping the organist with his swarm, he discovers quite the opposite and also makes other exciting discoveries among the cathedral towers. Subsequent Choir School novels are *Chorister's Cake, Cathedral Wednesday* and *Words and Music*.

Several of his other books are set in the Yorkshire Dales, where he spent his own childhood and where he worked for a time as a schoolteacher. He has also worked for the BBC, although he has mostly been a full time writer. Altogether he has produced more than twenty books for children, including *A Grass Rope*, *Earthfasts* and *Ravensgill*. He has also edited a number of anthologies.

Most of his stories are for older children, who are better able to appreciate the clever way he evokes place and atmosphere, as in A HAUNTED TERRACE and A PRINCE IN THE BUILDING, and his brilliant characterisation, of which THE TEST is a particularly good example. This story first appeared, in fact, in an anthology for adult readers.

William Mayne lives in the village of Thornton Rust in his beloved Yorkshire. He does all his writing and a great deal of reading in his comfortable stone cottage overlooking the Fells.

A Prince in the Building

by William Mayne

This is what I did. My name is Ethel March, I was younger then. I remember the time of year, it was the spring, because that was when we moved. Da knew about it before, of course, and he said March, March, march. He meant it was the month of March, and the second March was his own name because he was talking to himself but so that we could hear, and the third march was what we had to do, march away from our old place to a new one.

We used to have one room for all three of us, and we had to wait for a house since I was born, eleven years. Da said it was long enough, but there were worse places than our room. He had made it very nice and my corner had striped wallpaper, and I could sit on the bed and pull down a flap from the wall to put things on, but I couldn't keep it down because it was just over my pillow, and I couldn't lie the other way because my clothes were there. But I made a little shelf in the wall, where Da and Ma couldn't see, to put very small things in, the plastic things out of the bubble-gum machine were the right size. Sometimes in those machines you get two bubble-gums, and sometimes you get one, usually one, but sometimes you get a little plastic doll or some tiny false teeth or a model of a bicycle instead, and worst of all you sometimes get two plastic things and no bubble-gum.

I dug the little shelf out with a spoon, at night, and Da would think a mouse was nibbling the wood in the floor, and Ma put herself close together in case the mouse came to her. I left the wallpaper so that it made a little curtain over the shelf, and nobody saw it.

Our room was up two flights of stairs, and there were seven more rooms like it on the landing, and the stairs went up twice more, so we were halfway up. If you went upstairs again and looked out of the windows there you could see mountains a long way off, and too much sky. From our window we could see the next building, which was called Chapel Place. Our building was called Clover Hill. They were both made of bricks that were nearly shiny, but not quite. In the rain they got all patchy, and they were very dirty. Da didn't like our view much, but he said we had to be patient. I don't mind about the view, and Ma doesn't either, but I liked to go upstairs and look at the mountains and think of going there and sitting in the sunshine like magazine people. Inside our door Da had put a piece of wallpaper with real velvet stripes, red, and when our door was open a little bit, from outside it looked like a magazine room. Inside it was all furniture. Da said it was better to have too much, because one day we would have a house, or a bigger place.

The upstairs window belonged to a boy called Mortimer. He had a brother Steven a lot older, about seventeen, and only a mother, his Da wasn't there. Mortimer used to like looking at the mountains if it wasn't too smoky, because if it was, you couldn't see anything much, because on one side was Chapel Place and on the other the engine shed, and that was where the smoke came from. If he couldn't see the mountains he liked to lean out and look at the engines.

One day he said, "Ethel, would you like to be a queen?"

I said I would, and wear good shoes and go about in a car.

"You might, one day," he said. "Don't you tell Mamsy, or Steven, but I think I'm really a prince."

Mamsy was what he called his Ma. I said Steven ought to be a prince, too, but Mortimer said he wasn't really one of that family at all, but got left by accident in Clover Hill when he was a baby, to be brought up by Mamsy. "One day I shall go and find out where I'm prince of," he said. "But if I go now the catcher will come." The catcher is the man who wants to know why you aren't at school. He doesn't come for me, but Mortimer said he used to come for Steven. Mortimer liked to go to school, to learn everything so that he would be ready for being a prince. He often used to talk about it. He thought the mountains might be where he was prince of, because they were not in England. Steven told him that, but Mortimer didn't say anything about being a prince.

He thought I could be queen when he got to be king, and one day he gave me a sort of necklace, which was a silver chain and a blue jewel like glass hanging in the middle of it. The chain was broken near the catch, so I couldn't wear it, but he said it was to keep secret, and it was a crown jewel, so the queen and I had got crown jewels, only she had more than me.

I kept it secret, and I put it on my little shelf with the bubble-gum things behind the wallpaper.

There wasn't anything I could do with it, so it just stayed there. Mortimer got princier than he was before. He was thin, like a prince, not fat like Steven or their Mamsy. Mortimer got through the exam, and I didn't. Steven hit him all down the stairs, one flight, for boasting about it. Steven didn't pass his exam at all, and Mortimer was being too princy about it, I thought, but he was better the next day and said he had only passed it because he was a prince, which he couldn't help being. He said he would rather have gone to Park End, where I would have to go, but it was the divine right of kings to do what they were told. We had just done divine right, so I knew what he meant. It means that if you are a king you must be one, in spite of what people say, even if they cut your head off, and that is against the law in any case.

It was about a term before we moved that I went to Park End, and Mortimer to Gough Street, which is all boys. He had some of his prince idea taken away. Sometimes he told me he wondered whether he was a prince or not, because the other boys were so good at things, and they oughtn't to be better than a prince. He gave me another crown jewel, a ring, with a red stone in it. He said it was a ruby, and it was part of his father's treasure, not his father in Clover Hill, who was away still, but his father a king. He wouldn't ever show me what else he had. I put the ring with my other things, and looked at it at night, and once I washed it when Ma was out, and made it cleaner. There was earth in it under the claws that held the jewel. I thought it was like an eagle's foot, and Mortimer said the eagles lived in the mountains.

Steven went away about then, like his father. Mortimer said the police asked him to go to do something for them rather secret. He didn't want to go, because he was busy. Mortimer said he had to in the end, and his Mamsy was very upset about it and hoped he didn't come to any harm.

"I've got to look after her now," said Mortimer. "She's been a good mother to me. I will let her stay in the palace if she wants. Steven won't want to come."

They took down all of Chapel Place that term. They did it all when I was at school. When I came back they would be tidying up their shed and the watchman would be lighting his fire. Sometimes in the morning I would see them putting chains on to a wall, and in the evening when I came back the wall would be gone. Ma said the noise all day was terrible, and so was the dust, and she couldn't see what they were doing, because the last wall they took down was the end one next to Clover Hill.

Then it all got bright in our room, and I could see the mountains myself; I only had to sit up in bed and there they were over the

sink. But the sunlight would get in, and Ma thought it would make the covers fade, but Da would take the curtain down and sit in the sun. It didn't come very often.

Chapel Place was taken away, every brick, in lorries, and there was a great big place for games, and only the watchman there on Sundays and he couldn't send us away. They put up a fence later, and the boys would climb it just the same and make it into a zoo. We got a lot more noise into the room with the wall out of the way. Da said it would be Clover Hill next, good riddance. One day Ma was in a state when I got back, and so was Mortimer's Mamsy. The housing man had come round and told them to go on Saturday and look at new places, because it was Clover Hill next. Ma showed me how they were going to build a new Clover Hill and Chapel Place all in one, but not straight on to the buildings that had been there. When she showed me I could see the plan of it, because they had begun to build the new building, but only in the ground. They were waiting to take ours down before going any further.

Da was top pleased. He and Ma went round on Saturday first thing. They said I couldn't go and get in the way. Mortimer's Mamsy went as well, but not with them. Mortimer stayed with his homework, and I went to see him, but he was too busy about some work to bother with me, so I went down and cleaned up the room.

Da came back still top pleased. He said he was a moving man. Ma said she'd always lived in Clover Hill and got used to it, and what if the lifts got stuck? I wanted to live in a house with lifts in it, and Ma said in thirty years she never spent more than fifteen nights out of Clover Hill at a time.

"Go on, Ma," said Da. "It's a palace. I've been all over the world, and I can tell." He used to be a soldier, once, so he had seen a lot of places.

Ma said she was bound to go, and Da got even toppier, and we went to the pictures, and on Sunday we walked right across the town and looked at the new place. It was a much bigger building than Clover Hill, and the bricks were not at all shiny, and it didn't look patchy, though it rained a bit when we got there. Da and Ma couldn't remember which windows we were going to have. There were a lot of them, anyway, and they looked out three ways, north, south and west, and Da said he could lie in bed all Sunday and look at the mountains, but I couldn't see them from the ground. There were trees round the building.

"Six rooms," said Da. "Seventeen windows. Hot and cold water, too."

Ma liked that, because she'd only used a hot tap twice, but I knew them at school. She liked the windows, too, because she wanted to make curtains for them. We had to go in three weeks' time, in March. The building wasn't quite finished. They had done all the outside, but the inside hadn't been finished.

Mortimer's Mamsy had chosen a different place. She wanted to live on the ground, and there wasn't a ground place in this building. Its address was Hastings Court. and there were other battles near, all in the same grass.

We went back by bus, and Ma felt better when she had had a cup of tea. She didn't know what it would be like to have six rooms. The new place was as big as all our landing put together. Da said the bathroom was as big as our room, nearly, and we wouldn't have to share. That was a good thing, because I wouldn't have to wait until I got to school any more.

On Monday Da went round to the removal people and arranged for them to come on the proper day, a Tuesday.

Other people began to go before we did, because their places were ready. They weren't all going to Hastings Court though. Some were going to other battles, and some to other kinds of places. Some old people who hardly ever went out because of the stairs went to some littler places than ours, with lifts just the same, and they all liked it, even Ma, when she saw them all going. She had only seen the new place with nobody in it, and she liked people round about. Da told her there would be plenty in Hastings Court, and she began to like the idea a lot. She would rather do without taps than without people, and she didn't mind about the view, and she could put curtains up to stop the fading sun.

Mortimer and his Mamsy were going to a place called Abbey Stand. He said there was a wood near it. They were going to have the removal van straight after us: Da had arranged that, too, to help them. We were going to be the last people out of our staircase, and it got quieter and quieter, until we knew in the end that the person walking past could only be Mortimer, because no one else came now. Da thought we ought to practise living in more rooms than one, seeing that all the others were empty, but Ma wouldn't let him. I would have liked to practise, too, but Ma said wait until we had our own front door.

Mortimer said, one day, that he didn't know whether I would be queen after all. I didn't mind, because it would be two days to the moving one. He thought the king that was his father might come back and look for him in Clover Hill, and find it wasn't there any more, but I thought that Mortimer could go and look for the kingdom by then, and save the king the trouble. Mortimer took my address, and I took his, but not to write to each other, except when he developed into a prince, and then he went back to his homework, because he had that even when they were in the middle of removing.

When you move you can have the morning off. It often happened to people at Park End. Sometimes they moved in the afternoon and had that off instead. The van came early, and Da

33

was still all white shaving lather, but the man said he wasn't going to take the sink, so carry on, and Da did, and Ma packed away his towel all damp and Da put on his tie to give a hand, and in no time at all our room was in the van. Da and Ma got in the cab with the driver, and I got in the back and sat on the carpet. The tacks were sticking out still, but I got between them, and we went away. If you go in the back of a van things seem to follow you, and Clover Hill stayed with my eyes for a long time, until I found it had got smaller whilst I looked at it, and there were other things to see.

The new place was big, but not so big as our classrooms. I thought it would be, but I was glad it wasn't, or our furniture would never have been seen for space.

"Those windows want a rub up," said Ma, and began it straight away, using the sink in the kitchen as if she'd always had one, turning on the taps easily and getting the water. Da went back with the man to help Mortimer and his Mamsy, and Ma and I assorted ourselves out. I had a room to myself, and I could sit in it all alone, on the bed or on the floor, but Da would buy me a chair one day, Ma said.

Da had only half a morning off, so we didn't see him until the evening. He came in and walked about and said he couldn't believe it, and Ma said they were nice people next door, and they had a dog. Da said "Ah," and we said we had to have a dog, and Da agreed, but we couldn't have one yet.

So I went to bed for the first time, and I woke up early, and I wanted to look at the crown jewels, and I wondered how Mortimer was going on, but there was no little shelf of jewels and plastic things from the bubble-gum. I had quite forgotten to bring them with me, and they were still behind the wallpaper, and I thought Mortimer would think it was awful not to have them.

We didn't know where to have breakfast, there were so many rooms, and we had it in the kitchen in the end, because we still only had one table and it was there. Then I went off, and I had to go a new way to Park End, by bus, and there was a mist near all the battle buildings, and hundreds of sunrises in the windows.

I came back a different way, and when I got to Clover Hill, because I was going there to get the crown jewels, they were beginning to take it down, but I dodged round and went up our old

staircase. There was light in it, because the roof had begun to be off that very day. I went up to our room, and got the crown jewels and the plastic things, and just as I came out again somebody came running down from upstairs. I was going to go back into our room, but I saw it was Steven, Mortimer's brother, and somebody following him, running downstairs.

"Hey, Ethel," said Steven, speaking quietly although he said Hey, "you keep this and give it to Mortimer. I'm off," and he ran on downstairs.

He had given me a very bright thing, all made of jewels, white ones, like diamonds. It was a sort of crown, only it didn't join at the back. I only looked at it for a moment, and then I put it behind me, because a man had run downstairs, looking all round him.

"Where's he gone?" he said, and then ran on downstairs himself, because he seemed to have heard Steven go right down. I went down after him, and there were men holding Steven, and one was saying that there was nothing there but they'd look again. I thought they must be after the crown, so I put it under my coat, but it bulged, so I put it on my leg and held it through my skirt, and walked past. The crown was cold, and it was dreadful in the bus, but all right in the lift, I'm glad it wasn't stairs. The next day I wrapped it up, because it must be Mortimer's, not mine, and took it to his house after school. He said it was his crown and that was how he proved he was a prince, and put it away in a box. I haven't seen him since.

Ma told me the other day, now I'm older, what it was all about. Mortimer's father had all the jewels from another man, who had really stolen them, and Mortimer's father got into trouble for it, but no one knew where the jewels were. Steven got into trouble because he found them and tried to sell one. When he heard that Clover Hill was being taken down he came back to hide the rest away, but they caught him, but I had the jewels. The ones that Mortimer gave me were the same lot, and I've still kept them. I think Mortimer was a prince and they were his jewels. We have got a dog. Da called him Prince, and I agreed.

John Wyndham

John Wyndham was born in 1903 and spent his early childhood in Edgbaston, Birmingham. He first started writing short stories on a commercial basis in 1925 and under various pseudonyms contributed to many American magazines. When he resumed writing after the Second World War, he decided to explore the possibilities of science fiction. Between then and his death in 1969 he became one of the most respected exponents of the genre.

Although always exciting, his science fiction stories are more than just adventure yarns. They also look at the customs and attitudes of present-day society. The normal situation is in some way disturbed and we are then shown how well conventional values stand up to new stresses.

In *The Day of the Triffids,* his first and probably best known novel, the disturbance is caused by a disaster that blinds all but a few of the world's population. The resulting chaos is made even worse by the presence of triffids, grotesque, walking plants with a lethal sting. In *The Kraken Wakes,* the disturbance stems from an invasion by an alien form of life, which takes up residence in the deepest parts of the world's oceans. *The Chrysalids* deals with the persecution of mutants in a puritanical community founded by a few survivors of a world-wide nuclear war. *The Midwich Cuckoos* is the name given to describe a group of mysterious children, vastly superior in intelligence and willpower and with the ability to share one another's thoughts. METEOR comes from *The Seeds of Time,* a collection of ten stories which the author described as "experiments in adapting the s.f. motif to various styles of short story".

Meteor

by John Wyndham

The house shook, the windows rattled, a framed photograph slipped off the mantel-shelf and fell into the hearth. The sound of a crash somewhere outside arrived just in time to drown the noise of the breaking glass. Graham Toffts put his drink down carefully, and wiped the spilt sherry from his fingers.

"That sort of thing takes you back a bit," he observed. "First instalment of the new one, would you think?"

Sally shook her head, spinning the fair hair out a little so that it glistened in the shaded light.

"I shouldn't think so. Not like the old kind, anyway—they used to come with a sort of double-bang as a rule," she said.

She crossed to the window and pulled back the curtain. Outside there was complete darkness and a sprinkle of rain on the panes.

"Could have been an experimental one gone astray?" she suggested.

Footsteps sounded in the hall. The door opened, and her father's head looked in.

"Did you hear that?" he asked, unnecessarily. "A small meteor, I fancy. I thought I saw a dim flash in the field beyond the orchard." He withdrew. Sally made after him. Graham, following more leisurely, found her firmly grasping her father's arm.

"No!" she was saying, decisively. "I'm not going to have my dinner kept waiting and spoiled. Whatever it is, it will keep."

Mr. Fontain looked at her, and then at Graham.

"Bossy; much too bossy. Always was. Can't think what you want to marry her for," he said.

After dinner they went out to search with electric lamps. There was not much trouble in locating the scene of the impact. A small crater, some eight feet across, had appeared almost in the middle of the field. They regarded it without learning much, while Sally's terrier, Mitty, sniffed over the newly turned earth. Whatever had caused it had presumably buried itself in the middle.

"A small meteorite, without a doubt," said Mr. Fontain. "We'll set a gang on digging it out tomorrow."

Extract from Onns' Journal:

As an introduction to the notes which I intend to keep, I can scarcely do better than give the gist of the address given to us on the day preceding our departure from Forta* by His Excellency Cottafts. In contrast to our public farewell, this meeting was deliberately made as informal as a gathering of several thousands can be.

His Excellency emphasised almost in his opening words that though we had leaders for the purposes of administration, there was, otherwise, no least amongst us.

"There is not one of you men and women† who is not a volunteer," looking slowly round his huge audience. "Since you are individuals, the proportions of the emotions which led you to volunteer may differ quite widely, but, however personal, or however altruistic your impulses may have been, there is a common denominator for all—and that is the determination that our race shall survive.

"Tomorrow the Globes will go out.

"Tomorrow, God willing, the skill and science of Forta will break through the threats of Nature.

"Civilisation is, from its beginning, the ability to coordinate and direct natural forces—and once that direction has been started, it must be constantly maintained. There have been other dominant species on Forta before ours: they were not civilised, they did not direct Nature: they dwindled and died as conditions changed. But we, so far, have been able to *meet* conditions as they have changed, and we flourish.

"We flourish, moreover, in such numbers as undirected Nature could never have sustained. In the past we have surmounted problem after problem to make this possible, but now we find ourselves faced with the greatest problem yet. Forta, our world, is becoming senile, but we are not. We are like spirits that are still young, trapped in a failing body ...

"For centuries we have kept going, adapted, substituted, patched, but now the trap is closing faster, and there is little left to

---

* Onns gives no clues to Forta's position, nor as to whether it is a planet, a moon, or an asteroid.
† The terms "men" and "women" are not used biologically, but in the sense of the dominant species referring to its own members.

prop it open with. So it is now, while we are still healthy and strong, that we must escape and find ourselves a new home.

"I do not doubt that great-grandchildren of the present generation's great-grandchildren will be born on Forta, but life will be harder for them: they will have to spend much more labour simply to keep alive. That is why the Globes must go now, while we have strength and wealth to spare.

"And for you who go in them—what? Even guesses are vain. The Globes will set out for the four corners of the heavens, and where they land they may find anything—or nothing. All our arts and skills will set you on your courses. But, once you have left, we can do no more than pray that you, our seed, will find fruitful soil."

He paused, lengthily. Then he went on:

"Your charge you know, or you would not have offered yourselves. Nevertheless, it is one which you will not be able to learn too well, nor teach too often. In the hands of each and every one of you lies a civilisation. Every man and woman of you is at once the receptacle and the potential fountain of all that Forta signifies. You have the history, the culture, the civilisation of a planet. Use it. Use it well. Give it to others where it will help. Be willing to learn from others, and improve it if you can. Do not try to preserve it intact; a culture must grow to live. For those who cling too fondly to the past there is likely to be no future. Remember that it is possible that there is no intelligence elsewhere in the universe, which means that some of you will hold a trust not only for our race, but for all conscious life that may evolve.

"Go forth, then. Go in wisdom, kindliness, peace, and truth.

"And our prayers will go out with you into the mysteries of space...."

... I have looked again through the telescope at our new home. Our group is, I think, lucky. It is a planet which is neither too young nor too old. Conditions were better than before, with less cloud over its surface. It shines like a blue pearl. Much of the part I saw was covered with water—more than two-thirds of it, they tell me, is under water. It will be good to be in a place where irrigation and water supply are not one of the main problems of life. Nevertheless, one hopes that we shall be fortunate enough to make our landing on dry ground or there may be very great difficulties. . . .

I looked, too, at some of the places to which other Globes are bound, some small, some large, some new, with clouded surfaces that are a mystery. One at least is old, and iñ not much better case than our own poor Forta—though the astronomers say that it has the ability to support life for several millions of years. But I am glad that our group is going to the blue, shining world; it seems to beckon us, and I am filled with a hope which helps to quieten my fears of the journey.

Not that fears trouble me so much now; I have learnt some fatalism in the past year. I shall go into the Globe, and the anaesthetic gas will lull me to sleep without my being aware of it. When I wake again it will be on our shimmering new world. . . . If I do not wake, something will have gone wrong, but I shall never know that. . . .

Very simple, really—if one has faith. . . .

This evening I went down to look at the Globes; to see them objectively for the last time. Tomorrow, in all the bustle and preparation there will be no time for reflection—and it will be better so.

What a staggering, amazing—one had almost said impossible—work they are! The building of them has entailed labour beyond computation. They look more likely to crush the ground and sink into Forta herself than to fly off into space. The most massive things ever built! I find it almost impossible to believe that we can have built thirty of these metal mountains, yet there they stand, ready for tomorrow. . . .

And some of them will be lost. . . .

Oh, God, if ours may survive, let us never forget. Let us show ourselves worthy of this supreme effort. . . .

It can well be that these are the last words I shall ever write. If not, it will be in a new world and under a strange sky that I continue. . . .

"You shouldn't have touched it," said the Police Inspector, shaking his head. "It ought to have been left where it was until the proper authorities had inspected it."

"And who," enquired Mr. Fontain, coldly, "are the proper authorities for the inspection of meteors?"

"That's beside the point. You couldn't be sure it was a meteor, and these days a lot of other things besides meteors can fall out of the sky. Even now you've got it up you can't be sure."

"It doesn't look like anything else."

"All the same, it should have been left to us. It might be some device still on the Secret List."

"The Police, of course, knowing all about things on the Secret List?"

Sally considered it time to break in.

"Well, we shall know what to do next time we have a meteor, shan't we? Suppose we all go and have a look at it? It's in the outhouse now, looking quite unsecret."

She led the way round to the yard, still talking to stave off a row between the Inspector and her father.

"It only went a surprisingly short way down, so the men were soon able to get it out. And it turned out to be not nearly as hot as we'd expected, either, so they could handle it quite easily."

"You'd not say 'quite easily' if you'd heard the language they used about the weight of it," observed her father.

"It's in here," Sally said, leading the party of four into a musty, single-storey shed.

The meteor was not an impressive sight. It lay in the middle of the bare board floor; just a rugged, pitted, metallic-looking sphere something over two feet in diameter.

"The only kind of weapon that it suggests to me is a cannon-ball," said Mr. Fontain.

"It's the principle," retorted the Inspector. "We have standing orders that any mysterious falling object is to remain untouched until it has been examined by a War Office expert. We have already informed them, and it must not be moved again until their man has had a look at it."

Graham, who had hitherto taken no part, stepped forward and put his hand on it.

"Almost cold now," he reported. "What's it made of?" he added, curiously.

Mr. Fontain shrugged.

"I imagine it's just an ordinary chunk of meteoric iron. The only odd thing about it to me is that it didn't come down with more of a bump. If it were any kind of secret weapon, it would certainly be an exceedingly dull one."

"All the same, I shall have to give orders that it is not to be moved until the W.O. man has seen it," said the Inspector.

They started to move back into the yard, but on the threshold he paused.

"What's that sizzling sound?" he enquired.

"Sizzling?" repeated Sally.

"Kind of hissing noise. Listen!"

They stood still, the Inspector with his head a little on one side. Undeniably there was a faint, persistent sound on a note just within the range of audibility. It was difficult to place. By common impulse they turned back to regard the ball uneasily. Graham hesitated, and then stepped inside again. He leaned over the ball, his right ear turned down to it.

"Yes," he said. "It is."

Then his eyes closed, and he swayed. Sally ran forward and caught him as he sagged. The others helped her to drag him out. In the fresh air he revived almost immediately.

"That's funny. What happened?" he asked.

"You're sure the sound is coming from that thing?" asked the Inspector.

"Oh, yes. Not a doubt about it."

"You didn't smell anything queer?"

Graham raised his eyebrows: "Oh, gas, you mean. No, I don't think so."

"H'm," said the Inspector. He turned a mildly triumphant eye on the older man. "Is it usual for meteors to sizzle?" he enquired.

"Er—I really don't know. I shouldn't think so," Mr. Fontain admitted.

"I see. Well, in the circumstances I suggest that we all withdraw—preferably to a well-shielded spot on the other side of the house, just in case—while we wait for the expert," announced the Inspector.

Extract from Onn's Journal:

I am bewildered. I have just woken. But has it happened—or have we failed to start? I cannot tell. Was it an hour, a day, a year, or a century ago that we entered the Globe? No, it cannot have been an hour ago; I am sure of that by the tiredness of my limbs, and the way my body aches. We were warned about that:

"You will know nothing," they said, "nothing until it is all over. Then you will feel physically weary because your bodies will have been subjected to great strains. That should pass quite soon, but we shall give you some capsules of concentrated food and stimulants to help you overcome the effects more quickly."

I have taken one capsule, and I begin to feel the benefit of it already, but it is still hard to believe that it is over.

It seems such a short time ago that we climbed the long passage into the interior of the Globe and dispersed as we had been instructed. Each of us found his or her elastic compartment, and crawled into it. I released the valve to inflate the space between the inner and outer walls of my compartment. As the lining distended I felt myself lifted on a mattress of air. The top bulged down, the sides closed in, and so, insulated from shock in all directions, I waited.

Waited for what? I still cannot say. One moment, it seems, I lay there fresh and strong: the next, I was tired and aching.

Only that, to indicate that one life has ended and a new one is about to begin. My compartment has deflated. The pumps have been exchanging the gas for fresh air. That must mean that we are now on that beautiful, shining blue planet, with Forta only a speck in our new heavens.

I feel different for knowing that. All my life hitherto has been spent on a dying planet where our greatest enemy was lethal discouragement. But now I feel rejuvenated. There will be work, hope and life here: a world to build, and a future to build it for....

I can hear the drills at work, cutting a way out for us. What, I wonder, shall we find? We must watch ourselves closely. It may be easier for us to keep faith if we face hardships than if we find ourselves among plenty. But, whatever this world is like, faith *must* be kept. We hold a million years of history, a million years of knowledge, that *must* be preserved.

Yet we must also, as His Excellency said, be ready to adapt ourselves. Who can tell what forms of life may already exist here? One could scarcely expect to find real consciousness on a planet so young, but there may be the first stirrings of intelligence here. We must watch for them, seek them out, cultivate them. They may be quite different from us, but we must remember that it is their world, and help them where we can. We must keep in mind that it would be a wicked thing to frustrate even an alien form of life, on its own planet. If we find any such beings, our task must be to teach, to learn, to co-operate with them, and perhaps one day we may achieve a civilisation even greater than Forta's own....

"And just what," enquired the Inspector, "do you think you're doing with that, Sergeant Brown?"

The police-sergeant held the limp, furry body dangling by its tail.

"It's a cat, sir."

"That's what I meant."

"Well, I thought the W.O. gentleman might want to examine it, sir."

"What makes you think the War Office is interested in dead cats, Sergeant?"

The sergeant explained. He had decided to risk a trip into the outhouse to note developments, if any. Bearing in mind the Inspector's suggestion of gas, he had tied a rope round his waist so that he could be dragged back if he were overcome, and crawled in, keeping as low as possible. The precautions had proved unnecessary, however. The hissing or sizzling had ceased, and the gas had evidently dispersed. He had been able to approach the ball

without feeling any effects whatever. Nevertheless, when he had come so close to it that his ear was almost against it he had noticed a faint buzzing.

"Buzzing?" repeated the Inspector. "You mean sizzling."

"No, sir, buzzing." He paused, searching for a simile. "The nearest thing, to my mind, would be a circular saw, but as you might hear it from a very long way off."

Deducing from this that the thing, whatever it was, was still active, the sergeant had ordered his constables away to cover on the far side of an earth bank. He himself had looked into the shed from time to time during the next hour and a half, but observed no change.

He had noticed the cat prowl into the yard just as they were settling down to a snack of sandwiches. It had gone nosing round the shed door, but he had not bothered about it. Half an hour later, when he had finished his meal and cigarette, he had gone across to take another look. He had discovered the cat lying close to the "meteor." When he brought it out, he had found it was dead.

"Gassed?" asked the Inspector.

The sergeant shook his head. "No, sir. That's what's funny about it".

He laid the cat's body on top of a convenient wall, and turned the head to expose the under side of the jaw. A small circle of the black fur had been burnt away, and in the centre of the burn was a minute hole.

"H'm," said the Inspector. He touched the wound, and then sniffed at his forefinger. "Fur's burnt, all right, but no smell of explosive fumes," he said.

"That's not all, sir."

The sergeant turned the head over to reveal an exactly similar blemish on the crown. He took a thin, straight wire from his pocket, and probed into the hole beneath the jaw. It emerged from the other hole at the top of the head.

"Can you make anything of that, sir?" he asked.

The Inspector frowned. A weapon of minute bore, at point-blank range might have made one of the wounds. But the two appeared to be entrance and exit holes of the same missile. But a bullet did not come out leaving a neat hole like that, nor did it singe the hair about its exit. To all appearance, two of these microscopic bullets must have been fired in exactly the same line from above and below the head—which made no kind of sense.

"Have you any theories?" he asked the sergeant.

"Beats me, sir," the other told him.

"What's happening to the thing now? Is it still buzzing?" the Inspector enquired.

"No, sir. There wasn't a sound from it when I went in and found the cat."

"H'm," said the Inspector. "Isn't it about time that W.O. man showed up?"

Extract from Onns' Journal:

This is a terrible place! As though we were condemned to some fantastic hell. Can this be our beautiful blue planet that beckoned us so bravely? We cannot understand, we are utterly bewildered, our minds reel with the horror of this place. We, the flower of civilisation, now cower before the hideous monstrosities that face us. How can we ever hope to bring order into such a world as this?

We are hiding now in a dark cavern while Iss, our leader, consults to decide our best course. None of us envies him his responsibility. What provisions can a man make against not only the unknown, but the incredible? Nine hundred and sixty-four of us depend on him. There were a thousand: this is the way it happened.

I heard the drill stop, then there was a clanking as it was dismantled and drawn from the long shaft it had bored. Soon after that came the call for assembly. We crawled out of our compartments, collected our personal belongings, and met in the centre hall. Sunss, our leader then, himself called the roll. Everyone answered except four poor fellows who had not stood the strain of the journey. Then Sunss made a brief speech.

He reminded us that what had been done was irrevocable. No one yet knew what awaited us outside the Globe. If it should somehow happen that our party was divided, each group must elect its leader and act independently until contact with the rest was re-established.

"We need long courage, not brief bravery," he said. "Not heroics. We have to think of ourselves always as the seed of the future; and every grain of that seed is precious."

He hammered home the responsibility to all of us.

"We do not know, and we shall never know, how the other globes may have fared. So, not knowing, we must act as though we alone had survived, and as if all that Forta has ever stood for is in our hands alone."

It was he who led the way down the newly bored passage, and he who first set foot in the new land. I followed with the rest, filled with such a conflict of feelings as I have never known before.

And this world into which we have emerged: how can I describe it in all its alien qualities?

To begin with; it was gloomy and shadowed—and yet it was not night-time. Such light as there was came from a vast, grey panel hanging in the dusky sky. From where we stood it appeared trapezoid, but I suspect that was a trick of perspective, and that it was in fact a square, bisected twice, by two dark bars, into four smaller squares. In the murk over our heads it was possible to make out dimly-faint darker lines intersecting at strange angles. I could not guess at their significance.

The ground we stood on was like nothing I had known. It was a vast level plain, but ridged, and covered with small, loose boulders. The ridges were somewhat like strata that had been laid side by side instead of one on another. They lay all one way, disappearing into gloomy distance before and behind. Close beside us was a crevasse, as wide as my own height, also running either way, in a perfectly straight line. Some considerable distance beyond it was another, similar crevasse running exactly parallel to it, and beyond that a third, and an indication of a fourth.

The man beside me was nervous. He muttered something about a geometrical world lit by a square sun.

"Rubbish!" I told him shortly.

"Then how do you explain it?" he asked.

"I do not rush into swift, facile explanations," I told him. "I observe, and then, when I have gathered enough data, I deduce."

"What do you deduce from a square sun?" he asked, but I ignored him.

Soon we were all assembled outside the Globe, and waiting for Sunss to give directions. He was just about to speak when we were interrupted by a strange sound—a kind of regular soft padding, sometimes with a rasping scratch accompanying it. There was something ominous about it, and for a moment we were all frozen with apprehension—then, before we could move, the most fearsome monster emerged from behind our Globe.

Every historic traveller's tale pales beside the reality of the thing we faced. Never would I have believed that such a creature could exist had I not seen it for myself. The first we saw of it was an enormous face, thrusting round the side of the Globe, hanging in the air far above us. It was a sight to make the bravest shudder.

It was black, too, so that in the darkness it was difficult to be certain of its outline; but it widened across the top, and above the head itself one seemed to catch a glimpse of two towering pointed ears. It looked down on us out of two vast, glowing eyes set somewhat aslant.

It paused for a moment, the great eyes blinked, and then it came closer. The legs which then came into view were like massive pillars, yet they moved with a dexterity and control that was amazing in anything so vast. Both legs and feet were covered with close-set fibres that looked like strands of shining black metal. It bent its legs, lowering its head to look at us, and the fearful stench of its breath blew over us. The face was still more alarming at close quarters. It opened a cavern of a mouth; an enormous pink tongue flicked out and back. Above the mouth huge, pointed spines stood out sideways, trembling. The eyes which were fixed on us were cold, cruel, non-intelligent.

Until then we had been transfixed, but now panic took some of us. Those nearest to it fell back hurriedly, and at that one of the monstrous feet moved like lightning. A huge black paw with suddenly out-thrust claws smacked down. When it drew back, twenty of our men and women were no more than smears on the ground.

We were paralysed, all of us except Sunss. He, forgetting his instructions about personal safety, ran towards the creature. The great paw rose, hovered, and struck again. Eleven more fell at that second murderous blow.

Then I noticed Sunss again. He was standing right between the paws. His fire-rod was in his hands, and he was looking up at the monstrous head above him. As I watched, he lifted the weapon, and aimed. It seemed such folly against that huge thing, heroic folly. But Sunss was wiser than I. Suddenly the head jerked, a tremor shook the limbs, and without a sound the monster dropped where it stood.

And Sunss was under it. A very brave man. . . .

Then Iss took charge.

He decided that we must find a place of safety as soon as possible in case there were other such monsters lurking near. Once we had found that, we could start to remove our instruments and equipment from the Globe, and consider our next step. He decided to lead us forward down the broad way between two of the crevasses.

After travelling a considerable distance we reached the foot of a towering and completely perpendicular cliff with curiously regular rectangular formations on its face. At the base of it we found this cavern which seems to run a great distance both inwards and to both sides, and with a height that is oddly regular. Perhaps the man who spoke about a geometrical world was not so stupid as he seemed. . . .

Anyway, here we have a refuge from monsters such as that which Sunss killed. It is too narrow for those huge paws to reach, and even the fearful claws could only rake a little way inside.

Later. A terrible thing has happened! Iss and a party of twenty went exploring the cavern to see if they could find another way out other than on to the plain where our Globe lay.

Yes—lay! Past tense. That is our calamity.

After he had gone off, the rest of us waited, keeping watch. For some time nothing happened. Evidently and mercifully the monster had been alone. It lay in a great black mound where it had fallen, close to the Globe. Then a curious thing took place. More light suddenly poured over the plain. An enormous hooked object descended upon the slain monster, and dragged it away out of sight. Then there was a thunderous noise which shook everything about us, and the light dimmed again.

I do not pretend to explain these things: none of us can understand them. I simply do my best to keep a faithful record.

Another, much longer, period passed without any event. We were beginning to worry about what might have happened to Iss and his party for they had been a long time away, when almost the worst thing that could happen to us occurred without warning.

Again the plain became lighter. The ground beneath us set up a reverberating rumble and shook so violently to a series of shocks that we were hard put to keep on our feet. Peering out of the cavern I saw a sight that even now I can scarcely credit. Forms beside which our previous monster was insignificant: living, moving creatures reared up to three or four times the height of our vast Globe. I know this will not be believed—but it is the truth. Little wonder that the whole plain groaned and rumbled under the burden of four such. They bent over our Globe, they put their forelegs to it, and lifted it—yes, actually lifted that stupendous mass of metal from the ground. Then the shaking all about us became worse as they took its weight and tramped away on colossal feet.

The sight of that was too much for some of us. A hundred men ran out from our cavern, cursing, weeping, and brandishing their fire-rods. But it was too late, and the range was too great for them to do anything effective; besides, how could we hope to affect colossi such as these?

Now our Globe, with all its precious contents, is lost. Our inheritance is gone. We have nothing now; nothing, but our own few trifling possessions, with which to start building our new world....

It is bitter, bitter to have worked so hard and come so far, for this ....

Nor was that the only calamity. Only a little later two of Iss's companions came back with a dreadful tale.

Behind our cavern they had discovered a warren of broad tunnels, foul with the smell of unknown creatures and their droppings. They had made their way down them with difficulty. Several times they had been beset by different varieties of six-legged creatures, and sometimes eight-legged ones, all of horrible appearance. Many of these were a great deal larger than themselves, armed with fearful jaws and claws, and filled with a vicious ferocity which made them attack on sight. Terrifying though they looked, it soon became clear, however, that they were only really dangerous when they made unexpected attacks for they were non-sentient and the fire-rods made short work of them once they had been seen.

After a number of such encounters Iss had succeeded in reaching open country beyond the tunnels without the loss of a man. It had been when they were on the way back to fetch us that catastrophe had overtaken them. They had been attacked by fierce grey creatures about half the size of our first monster, which they guessed to be the builders of the tunnels. It was a terrible fight in which almost all the party perished before the monsters were overcome. Iss himself had fallen, and of all his men only these two had been left in a fit condition to make the journey back to the rest of us.

This new, ghastly tragedy is starting to sap our spirits, and our courage. . . .

We have chosen Muin as our new leader. He has decided that we must go forward, through the tunnels. The plain behind us is quite barren, our Globe is gone, if we stay here we shall starve; so we must try to get through to the open country beyond, trusting that Iss's sacrifice has not been in vain, and that there are no more grey monsters to attack us. . . .

God grant that beyond the tunnels this nightmare world gives place to sanity. . . .

Is it so much that we ask—simply to live, to work, to build, in peace . . . ?

Graham looked in to see Sally and her father a couple of days later.

"Thought you might like an interim report on your 'meteor,' " he said to Mr. Fontain.

"What was it, actually?" asked the older man.

"Oh, I don't say they've got that far. They've established that it was no meteor; but just what it really was still has them absolutely guessing. I'd got pretty curious by the time they decided to take it away, and after I'd talked big and waved my wartime status at them a bit, they consented to stretch a point and take me along, too. So you'd better grade this as confidential.

"When we went over the thing carefully at the research place it appeared to be simply a solid ball of some metal on which there's

58

been no report issued as yet. But in one place there was a hole, quite smooth, about half an inch in diameter, which went straight in, roughly to the middle. Well, they scratched their heads about the best way to tackle it, and decided in the end to cut it in half and see what. So they rigged up an automatic sawing device in a pit and set it going, and we all retreated to a reasonable distance, just in case. Now they're all a bit more puzzled than they were before!"

"Why, what happened?" Sally asked.

"Well, nothing actually *happened*. When the saw ran free we switched off and went back, and there was the ball lying in neat halves. But they weren't solid halves as we had expected. There *was* a solid metal rind about six inches thick, but then there was an inch or so of soft, fine dust, which has insulating qualities that seem to be interesting them quite a bit. Then inside a thinner metal wall was an odd formation of cells; more like a section of honeycomb than anything, only made of some flexible, rubbery material, and every one empty. Next, a belt about two inches wide, divided into metal compartments this time, all considerably larger than the cells in the outer part, and crammed with all sorts of things—packs of minute tubes, things that look like tiny seeds, different sorts of powders that have spilled about when the thing came apart, and which nobody's got around to examining properly yet, and finally a four-inch space in the middle separated into layers by dozens of paper-thin fins, and absolutely empty otherwise.

"So there is the secret weapon—and if you can make anything of that lot, I'm sure they'll be pleased to hear about it. Even the dust layer disappointed them by not being explosive. Now they're all asking one another what the hell such a thing could be remotely expected to do."

"That's disappointing. It seemed so like a meteor—until it started sizzling," said Mr. Fontain.

"One of them has suggested that in a way it may be. A sort of artificial meteor," Graham said. "That's a bit too fancy for the rest, though. They feel that if something could be sent across space at all, surely it would be something more intelligible."

"It would be exciting if it were," Sally said. "I mean, it would be such a much more hopeful thing than just another secret

59

weapon—a sort of sign that perhaps one day we shall be able to do it ourselves....

"Just think how wonderful it might be if we really could do that! Think of all the people who are sick to death of secret weapons, and wars, and cruelties, setting out one day in a huge ship for a clean, new planet where we could start again. We'd be able to leave behind all the things that make this poor old world get boggier and boggier. All we'd want is a place where people could live, and work, and build, and be happy. If we could only start again somewhere else, what a lovely, lovely world we might——" She stopped suddenly at the sound of a frenzied yapping outside. She jumped up as it changed to a long-drawn howl.

"That's Mitty!" she said. "What on earth——?"

The two men followed her out of the house.

"Mitty! Mitty!" she called, but there was no sign of the dog, nor sound from it now.

They made round to the left, where the sound had seemed to come from. Sally was the first to see the white patch lying in the grass beside the outhouse wall. She ran towards it, calling; but the patch did not move.

"Oh, poor Mitty!" she said, "I believe she's dead!"

She went down on her knees beside the dog's limp body.

"She *is*!" she said. "I wonder what——" She broke off abruptly, and stood up. "Oh, something's stung me! Oh, it *hurts*!" She clutched at her leg, tears of anguish suddenly coming into her eyes.

"What on earth——?" began her father, looking down at the dog. "What are all those things—ants?"

Graham bent down to look.

"No, they're not ants. I don't know what they are."

He picked one of the little creatures up and put it on the palm of his hand to look at it more closely.

"Never seen anything like that before," he said.

Mr. Fontain, beside him, peered at it, too.

It was a queer-looking little thing, under a quarter of an inch long. Its body seemed to be an almost perfect hemisphere with the flat side below and the round top surface coloured pink, and as shiny as a ladybird's wing-cases. It was insect-like, except that it

60

stood on only four short legs. There was no clearly defined head; just two eyes set in the edge of the shiny dome. As they watched, it reared up on two of its legs, showing a pale, flat underside, with a mouth set just below the eyes. In its forelegs it seemed to be holding a bit of grass or thin wire.

Graham felt a sudden, searing pain in his hand.

"Hell's bells!" he said, shaking it off. "The little brute certainly can sting. I don't know what they are, but they're nasty things to have around. Got a spray handy?"

"There's one in the scullery," Mr. Fontain told him. He turned his attention to his daughter. "Better?" he enquired.

"Hurts like hell," Sally said, between her teeth.

"Just hang on a minute till we've dealt with this, then we'll have a look at it," he told her.

Graham hurried back with the spray in his hand. He cast around and discovered several hundreds of the little pink objects crawling towards the wall of the outhouse. He pumped a cloud of insecticide over them and watched while they slowed, waved feeble legs, and then lay still. He sprayed the locality a little more, to make sure.

"That ought to fix 'em", he said. "Nasty, vicious little brutes. Never seen anything quite like them—I wonder what on earth they were?"

Saki

Saki (Hector Munro) was born in 1870 at Akyab in Burma, where his father was a senior official in the police force. His mother died when he was two years old and he was sent to England to live with two maiden aunts at Pitton in North Devon. He himself joined the Burma Police in 1893 but resigned a year later because of ill health. Although he subsequently became much sought after as a journalist, short story writer and conversationalist, he remained a rather lonely, detached man. When war broke out in 1914, he enlisted as a private, refused several times to accept a commission as an officer, and was an NCO in the Royal Fusiliers when he was killed in action at Beaumont-Hamel in France in 1916.

Children and animals feature frequently in his short stories and often provide the means for upsetting the values and manners of the middle-class Edwardian society in which he lived. This approach is used to particularly good effect in THE OPEN WINDOW and in *The Lumber Room,* in which young Nicholas gets the better of his pompous, domineering aunt and leaves her stuck in a rainwater tank for the afternoon. Such women were a favourite target for Saki's wit; it may well have been his way of taking revenge on the two fearsome aunts who looked after him as a boy.

Not all his stories are light-hearted, however. In *Sredni Vashtar* the cruel female guardian of ten-year-old Conradin meets a gruesome fate when she attempts to get rid of his pet, and in *The Interlopers* two bitter enemies, stranded in a Russian forest, at last become friends only to be killed by wolves shortly afterwards. These and other stories are available in a number of anthologies.

The Open Window

by Saki

"My aunt will be down presently, Mr. Nuttel," said a very self-possessed young lady of fifteen; "in the meantime you must try and put up with me."

Framton Nuttel endeavoured to say the correct something which should duly flatter the niece of the moment without unduly discounting the aunt that was to come. Privately he doubted more than ever whether these formal visits on a succession of total strangers would do much towards helping the nerve cure which he was supposed to be undergoing.

"I know how it will be," his sister had said when he was preparing to migrate to this rural retreat; "you will bury yourself down there and not speak to a living soul, and your nerves will be worse than ever from moping. I shall just give you letters of introduction to all the people I know there. Some of them, as far as I can remember, were quite nice."

Framton wondered whether Mrs. Sappleton, the lady to whom he was presenting one of the letters of introduction, came into the nice division.

"Do you know many of the people round here?" asked the niece, when she judged that they had had sufficient silent communion.

"Hardly a soul," said Framton. "My sister was staying here, at the rectory, you know, some four years ago, and she gave me letters of introduction to some of the people here."

He made the last statement in a tone of distinct regret.

"Then you know practically nothing about my aunt?" pursued the self-possessed young lady.

"Only her name and address," admitted the caller. He was wondering whether Mrs. Sappleton was in the married or widowed state. An undefinable something about the room seemed to suggest masculine habitation.

"Her great tragedy happened just three years ago," said the child; "that would be since your sister's time."

"Her tragedy?" asked Framton; somehow in this restful country spot tragedies seemed out of place.

"You may wonder why we keep that window wide open on an October afternoon," said the niece, indicating a large French window that opened on to a lawn.

"It is quite warm for the time of the year," said Framton; "but has that window got anything to do with the tragedy?"

"Out through that window, three years ago to a day, her husband and her two young brothers went off for their day's shooting. They never came back. In crossing the moor to their favourite snipe-shooting ground they were all three engulfed in a treacherous piece of bog. It had been that dreadful wet summer, you know, and places that were safe in other years gave way suddenly without warning. Their bodies were never recovered. That was the dreadful part of it." Here the child's voice lost its self-possessed note and became falteringly human. "Poor aunt always thinks that they will come back some day, they and the little brown spaniel that was lost with them, and walk in at that window just as they used to do. That is why the window is kept open every evening till it is quite dusk. Poor dear aunt, she has often told me how they went out, her husband with his white waterproof coat over his arm, and Ronnie, her youngest brother, singing, 'Bertie, why do you bound?' as he always did to tease her, because she said it got on her nerves. Do you know, sometimes on still quiet evenings like this, I almost get a creepy feeling that they will all walk in through that window—"

She broke off with a little shudder. It was a relief to Framton when the aunt bustled into the room with a whirl of apologies for being late in making her appearance.

"I hope Vera has been amusing you?" she said.

"She has been very interesting," said Framton.

"I hope you don't mind the open window," said Mrs. Sappleton briskly; "my husband and brothers will be home directly from shooting, and they always come in this way. They've been out for snipe in the marshes today, so they'll make a fine mess over my poor carpets. So like you men-folk, isn't it?"

She rattled on cheerfully about the shooting and the scarcity of birds, and the prospects for duck in the winter. To Framton it was all purely horrible. He made a desperate but only partially successful effort to turn the talk on to a less ghastly topic; he was conscious that his hostess was giving him only a fragment of her attention, and her eyes were constantly straying past him to the open window and the lawn beyond. It was certainly an unfortunate coincidence that he should have paid his visit on this tragic anniversary.

"The doctors agree in ordering me complete rest, an absence of mental excitement, and avoidance of anything in the nature of violent physical exercise," announced Framton, who laboured under the tolerably wide-spread delusion that total strangers and chance acquaintances are hungry for the least detail of one's ailments and infirmities, their cause and cure. "On the matter of diet they are not so much in agreement," he continued.

"No?" said Mrs. Sappleton, in a voice which only replaced a yawn at the last moment. Then she suddenly brightened into alert attention—but not to what Framton was saying.

"Here they are at last!" she cried. "Just in time for tea, and don't they look as if they were muddy up to the eyes!"

Framton shivered slightly and turned towards the niece with a look intended to convey sympathetic comprehension. The child was staring out through the open window with dazed horror in her eyes. In a chill shock of nameless fear Framton swung round in his seat and looked in the same direction.

In the deepening twilight three figures were walking across the lawn towards the window; they all carried guns under their arms, and one of them was additionally burdened with a white coat hung over his shoulders. A tired brown spaniel kept close at their heels. Noiselessly they neared the house, and then a hoarse young voice chanted out of the dusk: "I said, Bertie, why do you bound?"

Framton grabbed wildly at his stick and hat; the hall-door, the gravel-drive, and the front gate were dimly noted stages in his headlong retreat. A cyclist coming along the road had to run into the hedge to avoid imminent collision.

"Here we are, my dear," said the bearer of the white mackintosh, coming in through the window; "fairly muddy, but most of it's dry. Who was that who bolted out as we came up?"

"A most extraordinary man, a Mr. Nuttel," said Mrs. Sappleton; "could only talk about his illnesses, and dashed off without a word of good-bye or apology when you arrived. One would think he had seen a ghost."

"I expect it was the spaniel," said the niece calmly; "he told me he had a horror of dogs. He was once hunted into a cemetery somewhere on the banks of the Ganges by a pack of pariah dogs, and had to spend the night in a newly dug grave with the creatures snarling and grinning and foaming just above him. Enough to make anyone lose their nerve."

Romance at short notice was her speciality.

Eilís Dillon

Eilís (pronounced Eleesh) Dillon was born in 1920 in Galway, Eire. After attending the Ursuline Convent in Sligo, she started out to be a professional cellist but turned to writing instead. "I never remember a time when I did not want to write. I composed my first story at the age of seven, about a mouse called Harry who got into bad company, committed murder and was hanged."

As in BAD BLOOD, animals still feature in a number of her stories. *A Herd of Deer* tells how fifteen-year-old Peter Regan takes on the job of finding the deer which have mysteriously vanished from a rich landowner's herd. In *A Family of Foxes*, set on one of the Irish islands, Patsy and his friends rescue two grey foxes from the sea and keep them hidden from the other islanders, who hate all foxes. Authentic accounts of life on the Irish islands can also be found in: *The Coriander*, which is about a feud between the men of Inishthorav and the doctor they are holding prisoner; *The Sea Wall*, in which old Sally McDonagh's warning that a great wave will sweep over the island of Inisharcain is heeded only by her grandson and his friend; *The Singing Cave*, an exciting story about the discovery of a Viking relic on the island of Barrinish; and *The Cruise of the Santa Maria*, in which a sudden storm drives two young sailors to an unknown island with only one inhabitant.

Eilís Dillon, who is an authority on Anglo-Irish literature and speaks Gaelic, English, French and Italian, has produced more than twenty books for young readers as well as a number of novels for adults.

Bad Blood

by Eilís Dillon

In the early, early morning the lake was utterly still. John could see it from his bedroom window, laid out smoothly like a sheet of white satin, reflecting the white sky. Here and there, just above the surface, little puffs of mist floated. Each one certainly contained the spirit of a magician, just disappeared after his night's work. The lake was not wide here, so that he could see the tall thin reeds at the far side, motionless, doubling their length in the water below. The coots and water-hens were still asleep, or at least they had not yet come out to splash and paddle and scurry up and down at the edge of the reed-beds.

For the hundredth time, John wished he had a boat. With his father's land running down to the edge of the lake, it was never possible to forget the delights that he must miss. On such a morning as this, he would slide his boat into the water softly, so as not to disturb it with the smallest ripple. He could almost feel the boat grinding on the shingle, crushing with a dry crackling sound the hollow pieces of reed that lay everywhere along the shore, then floating erect and free. The keel would touch bottom for a moment at the bows as he stepped in, and then rise a little out of the water as he moved to the stern. A long gentle push with one oar would turn the bows out towards the middle of the lake. Then he would settle on the thwart and slide both oars into the stirrup-shaped rowlocks and move off, dipping as softly as a fishing swan, sending a great right-angular line washing away towards the shore.

But he had no boat. Mike Boyle, their neighbour in the next

farm, owned a boat, but John must never borrow it. There was bad blood between John's family and the Boyles, and John must always be very careful not to make matters worse. But they were already as bad as they could be, he thought, because the bad blood was directly responsible for the fact that John had no boat. There had been a lawsuit about boundaries and drainage, and it had cost so much that there could be no talk of boats until the lawyers had been paid. "Next year, perhaps," his father had said. Next year might come, John thought, but "next year perhaps" was a long way off.

A fish pushed his nose half an inch above the calm surface of the lake, sending a widening circle travelling slowly in every direction. Just as the centre of the circle became still, the fish jumped again, as if he had enjoyed the effect of what he had done the first time. John took a line from the drawer of his cupboard and examined it to see that it had a hook on the end. It was a home-made line. He had no fishing-rod, but the line would have been all right from a boat. On his quiet way out of the house he passed through the kitchen and collected the little wad of sour dough that he kept handy at all times. It was not that he meant to fish, but it just didn't seem right to go down to the lake without a line.

Everything was white this morning, even the dew on the grass, lying heavy in white beads, in a way that it never did after rain. He took off his sandals and brushed through the grass, expertly avoiding the occasional short, strong thistles. In a few hours this field would be a torment of horseflies, but now it was too early for them. Over by the single elm tree, the cattle were all clustered together, still lying half asleep in the wet grass. They were Kerry cows, great milkers, never complaining, and providing an endless supply of silky, big-eared calves as black as themselves, and with short, trembling tails. Some of the cows turned slow, friendly heads to look at him as he passed, but they did not get up.

The field ended at the edge of the lake, sloping steeply for the last few yards. The grass was cropped short here, for it was the favourite grazing ground of the cattle since the warm weather had begun. They liked to step into the lake and cool their feet, in the hot part of the day.

The boundary hedge between the two farms began to thin as it neared the shingle. When the hedge finished there was only a single wire, stretching from the last thorn bush to a stake planted out in the lake. It was a flimsy arrangement, but it served well enough.

The short pieces of dried reed tickled the soles of his feet. He hopped like a bird over the shingle, with bent knees and eyes down, watching for sharp stones. When he was standing in the ice-cold water so that it bit at his toes, he looked up at last.

Then he saw the heifer. Immediately, it seemed as if his blood stopped flowing, as if he would never breathe nor move again. He knew that heifer. She was a Jersey, and she belonged to Mike Boyle. He had a little herd of these beautiful animals. Secretly and with shame, John loved those cows as he had never loved his own. Everything about them was perfect, their pale brown colouring, shading to cream underneath, their elegant, bony bodies, their slow, intelligent faces and their gentle, confiding natures. John's greatest ambition was to own a herd of Jersey cattle, some wonderful day when he would have a farm of his own. He could see their rich yellow milk singing into big galvanised buckets. No one would ever milk them except himself, no one. Often he had peered unseen through the boundary hedge and had seen Mike Boyle carelessly herding his cattle home without love or interest. From these secret watchings, John knew every one of them as well as their owner did.

He recognised the heifer at once, though there was so little of her to be seen. She was far out in the lake, so far that only her long back and her uplifted, frightened head showed above the water. There she stood, quite motionless. Only for the unnatural upward tilt of her neck, one would have thought that she was enjoying a cooling bath. She was carrying her first calf, he knew. This was probably why she could not turn easily now and come ashore. He was quite certain that if no one came to her aid, she would stand there until she became exhausted and dropped into the water to drown. The thought made him a little sick.

He delayed no longer. A boat was necessary. If he had had a boat of his own he would have used it, but since he had not, he must use Boyle's boat. There it was, a strong, grey-painted one, lying drawn up just clear of the water line. He knew where the oars

were, stuck in a leafy thorn bush right near the boat.

In a flash he had skipped under the wire, not feeling the sharp stones on the soles of his feet now. He brought out the oars one by one, burying his face deep among the sweet, shining leaves of the whitethorn. First one and then the other went into the boat. Then he sent it sliding down across the shingle, crushing the hollow reed with a soft, dry, crackling sound. When the stern was well afloat he pushed off with a gentle oar so as not to frighten the heifer. He slid the oars into the rowlocks and began to row towards her.

She turned a huge, round, terrified eye on him when he came near.

"Silly little gom," he said softly. "Be quiet for just a minute more, just one minute."

Edging the boat near to her, he patted her wet neck once. Then he took the long mooring-rope that lay coiled in the bows of the boat, made a slip knot in the end of it and quickly passed it over one of her horns.

72

"And now, oh God in heaven, please don't let her stumble, for if she does she'll certainly drown. If Mike Boyle were to see me now, he might even think that I had led his heifer out into the lake to make an end of her."

He glanced uneasily towards Boyle's house, but there was no sign of life there, no smoke from the chimney and no sheepdog nosing around. His own house was quiet, too. It would be just as bad if his father were to come down to the edge of the lake and perhaps call out advice to him, frightening the heifer. John was determined that if he got that heifer ashore, he would never tell a soul about her adventure. He felt in his bones that as sure as he did, he would somehow be blamed for the whole affair.

He pulled gently on the rope. This had the effect of drawing the boat nearer to the heifer, so that her eyes widened still further. He let go of the rope at once. There was only one way to do it. He sat on the thwart, facing the bows of the boat, and took the oars in his hands. When he lifted them, the heifer jerked her head away in fright. He dropped the oars very slowly into the water and pulled once. First she just stretched her neck to follow the pull, and then she took one step.

"Come along, come along," he said coaxingly. "Patience and perseverance brought the snail to Jerusalem."

She took another step. A splash of water washed against her nostrils, so that she spluttered. He waited in agony while she tossed her head once. If she were to bellow now, Mike Boyle might come running. It would soon be getting-up time. Cows like music, he remembered. He sang a little song for her in Irish. It was one that he had learned at school, about a red-backed cow with a single horn. The heifer seemed pleased, and she took another step, with her eyes fixed on him. Now she had turned, so that she was facing the shore. She must not be hurried. She must not be frightened. One downward plunge of her head and she might never come up again.

Two more steps and her flanks showed a little above the water. Still she held her head high, though there were six inches now between her chin and the surface of the lake. Slowly, slowly he drew her along. The boat moved heavily, because it was travelling the wrong way, but it was a well-balanced boat. The heifer did not lift her feet high, and thus she was able to feel and avoid the bigger stones that lay in her path.

John glanced over the side from moment to moment. The sun had come up, and spiralling lines of light glittered downwards through the water. They picked out the white stones shadowed with brown mud. Now the heifer was coming a little faster as the water became shallow. Before the stern of the boat could touch on the shingle, he slid the oars aboard and hopped out into the water. The boat rocked, and sent a wave splashing against her knees, but it did not matter now. He slipped the knot off her horn and led her, holding the same horn, right up on to the grass. He waited for a moment then, almost as if he had expected her to thank him for his services, but she just swished her sodden tail and lumbered off. All at once she seemed to become furiously hungry, for she began to tear up huge mouthfuls of grass as if she had been starved for a week.

John was deeply satisfied. It hardly seemed right that he should not be rewarded for his intelligence and efficiency. He swaggered down to the edge of the lake again and suddenly stooped for a stone and sent it spinning off across the flat water, leaving a dozen rings in its trail as if a line of fishes had all jumped together.

He had to wade knee-deep to the boat, which had sat still exactly where he had left it. The mooring-rope was soaked. If Mike Boyle were to see it before it had time to dry, he would know that the boat had been used. John picked the rope out of the water and began to turn the bows towards the shore. Then he stopped. Here, of course, was his reward. He would go fishing. Not for long, because he must be back with the boat before breakfast, but long enough to try for that bold fish that had jumped twice in two minutes.

Four strokes of the oars took himself and the boat out of sight of Boyle's house, so that he could pause and take out his line and bait it with the dough, and drop it overboard from the stern. He might get a pike. They would snap at anything. Trout have more delicate tastes. No one would want to eat a pike, but if it were a big one, its size would make up for that. He would show it to the family at once, and then keep it to show to the boys in the evening. The trouble would be to put it in a place where the cats wouldn't

find it. That black cat Mulligan would nose out a fish half a mile away. Paddy the yardman swore that he had seen him fishing, but Paddy was a noted liar.

Hardly touching the water with the oars, John sent the boat sliding along, further and further away from home. The line trailed slackly. It should have had a fly on the end, he thought, if it were to catch a trout. Suddenly he realised that he did not care if he caught nothing, it was so pleasant just to float along under the white sky, watching the mist lift and flutter and blow away, and hearing the soft, dry, swinging song of the rushes all around him.

It was only by chance that his eye was on it when the line suddenly tightened. He let go of the oars and waited until there was a jerk. Within ten seconds he had plunged forward and flipped the fish into the boat. For a moment he was sorry for it as it panted for breath. Then when it lay still he was filled with a bursting triumph, that had to be let loose in a mighty yell. It was a trout, a huge one. It should only have liked flies, but it had accepted a bit of mouldy, sour dough and now it was his. He wished he could go sailing up and down that lake for ever, filling Mike Boyle's boat with mountains of monstrous fish until the water washed over the gunwale. But it was Mike's boat and it was time to return it.

He placed the trout carefully where he could see it. Then he turned the boat in a great swinging curve. The lake was so wide here that its further edge was only a blue-grey line. Another boat was coming towards him, a slow-moving black boat, probably from one of the remote villages up there by the lake-side. The people from those villages were as slow and as black as their boats. They wore black clothes and black hats, and they would scarcely look at you to pass the time of day as they rowed down towards the town. John had found them unfriendly and silent, too, when he had gone with his father in a hired boat to buy sheep from them. Now he measured the distance between himself and the other boat, and he was glad to see that he would have turned in towards the shore before the other would have come abreast of him. Thus occupied, he never once glanced behind him until he was almost ashore on the beach below Mike Boyle's house. And there, standing at the water's edge, so close that the toes of his huge boots were awash, was Mike Boyle himself.

Though his legs were short, his body seemed to have been made for a taller man, thick and strong and heavy about the neck and shoulders. His habit of leaning forward on the balls of his feet gave him a threatening appearance, as if he were always prepared to strike out with his ready fists. His eyes were small and piercing, and they seemed now to send out little deadly jets of venom, as he waited for the boat to come within his grasp.

He seized the point of the bows and jerked the boat roughly towards him, so that its keel rasped on the stones. John drew the oars aboard and laid them neatly under either gunwale. Then he picked up his trout and stepped out on to the shingle.

"Caught you," said Mike Boyle. "Caught you at last. Pinching my boat in the early morning to go fishing, thinking I wouldn't spot you. But the early bird catches the worm, and I've caught a worm this morning, all right."

"This is the first time I've borrowed the boat," said John.

"Borrowing without leave is stealing, young man," said Mike Boyle. "Didn't they teach you that at home?" He lifted one side of his upper lip. "Maybe they didn't, though. You can't teach something if you don't know it yourself."

Standing silently in front of Mike Boyle, John felt as if a volcano

were about to erupt inside him. It seemed as if he had suddenly grown two feet taller, so that he towered in the air over this little man's head, as if he had suddenly become strong enough to lift Mike Boyle by his thick bull neck and send him spinning through the air like a shrieking rainbow, until he landed in the middle of the lake with a splash that would sprinkle the sun. But the volcano died down again and he said:

"My father doesn't know I took the boat."

"But he'll know when you bring home that trout for his breakfast," said Mike Boyle. "And it will be all the sweeter because it was caught from my boat." He stuck out a hand whose fingers twitched with impatient energy. "Just give me that fish, young man. That will teach you better than any talk, not to steal my boat again."

John put the fish behind his back for safety.

"It's my fish," he said. "You won't get it. I caught it."

"You caught it from my boat, so it belongs to me."

"The fish belongs to the line, not to the boat."

"You'd never have caught that fish without my boat," said Mike Boyle contemptuously. "There's no one knows it better than yourself. That's why you had to get up at the crack of dawn, when you thought everyone would be asleep, and sneak down here like the thief you are."

If the Jersey heifer had not come rambling down to the edge of the lake just then, John might have held to his resolution of not telling how he had saved her life an hour ago. Now all at once he found that he could no longer bear the injustice of Mike Boyle's accusations. As he began to tell the story, it occurred to him that it might soften Mike Boyle's heart to hear it, as well as making him understand how John had come to borrow the boat. "Do good to them that hate you," John's father always said.

While he described how he had led the heifer step by step ashore, he watched Mike Boyle's face, how the eyebrows jerked and lifted, and at last there was even the beginnings of a sour smile. Swinging the fish easily in his left hand, John pointed with his right to the exact place where the heifer had stood. Mike Boyle's eye followed the pointing forefinger, and then dropped quickly, covetously, to the fish. The sour smile became a sour, snorting laugh.

"A little hero," he said. "You'd better go over at once and tell your story to Tom Burke, for I sold him that heifer last week. She's wandered back twice already. Maybe he'll make you a present of the calf as a reward. And now, just hand over that fish without any more talk."

This time, the twitching hand made a grab for the fish. Instinctively, John lifted it high out of his reach so that it dangled in the air between them. Then it seemed to him that it dwindled in size there before his eyes, that its scales no longer shone with the same lustre, that its soft, ribbed tail had become dry and ugly and stark. He thought of the bad blood, and he saw quite clearly that future generations of his own family and of the Boyles might some day curse this little fish, if he allowed it to stir up still further the ill feeling between them.

Slowly he lowered his arm and stretched it towards Mike Boyle. He could not bring himself to speak. Mike Boyle's little eyes narrowed, but though he put out his hand he did not take the trout at once. He paused for a moment and then snapped at it sharply, like a dog catching a fly. When it was gone, John felt serene and calm, as if he had done Mike Boyle a great service, or as if he had after all been the victor in spite of losing his fish.

Perhaps the same idea came to trouble Mike Boyle's satisfaction. John was astonished to see a look of hurt bewilderment replace the triumphant expression that he had had at the moment of success. Then all at once he was bellowing:

"Get off my land! I'll have the law on you! Get off! Get off!"

Grinning from ear to ear, John skipped under the flimsy wire into his own field, and started to run up the long slope towards home.

James Thurber

James Thurber was born in 1894 in Columbus, Ohio. From 1920 he worked as a journalist and was associated particularly with the *New Yorker* magazine, in which many of his prose pieces and cartoons first appeared. A boyhood accident deprived him of his sight in one eye and in later life the other eye also deteriorated. Although almost total blindness forced him to give up drawing in his last years, he continued to dictate stories and articles and even enjoyed acting in a stage version of his work a short while before his death in 1961.

You may have already read some of his books for younger children, such as: *The Thirteen Clocks,* which has all the classic ingredients of a fairy story—a princess in distress, a prince in disguise, a wicked uncle and a thrilling last-minute race between good and evil; *The Wonderful O,* which concerns two abominable villains who, in revenge for their lack of success in a treasure hunt, punish the gentle inhabitants of Coroo by banning everything with an O in it; *Many Moons,* about a little princess who wants the moon; and *The Great Quillow,* the story of a toymaker who saves his town from a giant. These books have been as popular with adults as they have with children.

If you enjoy THE SECRET LIFE OF WALTER MITTY, which tells of the heroic daydreams of a timid man (and was made into a film starring Danny Kaye), you can find more of his humorous stories and offbeat cartoons in *A Thurber Carnival.* Individual titles include: *My Life and Hard Times,* very funny anecdotes about his boyhood and early youth; *Fables for Our Times,* modern fables with some unusual conclusions; *The Seal in the Bedroom* and *The Owl in the Attic.*

The Secret Life of Walter Mitty

by James Thurber

"We're going through!" The Commander's voice was like thin ice breaking. He wore his full-dress uniform, with the heavily braided white cap pulled down rakishly over one cold grey eye. "We can't make it, sir. It's spoiling for a hurricane, if you ask me." "I'm not asking you, Lieutenant Berg," said the Commander. "Throw on the power lights! Rev her up to 8500! We're going through!" The pounding of the cylinders increased; ta-pocketa-pocketa-pocketa-*pocketa-pocketa*. The Commander stared at the ice forming on the pilot window. He walked over and twisted a row of complicated dials. "Switch on No. 8 auxiliary!" he shouted. "Switch on No. 8 auxiliary!" repeated Lieutenant Berg. "Full strength in No. 3 turret!" shouted the Commander. "Full strength in No. 3 turret!" The crew, bending to their various tasks in the huge, hurtling eight-engined Navy hydroplane, looked at each other and grinned. "The Old Man'll get us through," they said to one another. "The Old Man ain't afraid of Hell!" . . .

"Not so fast! You're driving too fast!" said Mrs. Mitty. "What are you driving so fast for?"

"Hmm?" said Walter Mitty. He looked at his wife, in the seat beside him, with shocked astonishment. She seemed grossly unfamiliar, like a strange woman who had yelled at him in a crowd. "You were up to fifty-five," she said. "You know I don't like to go more than forty. You were up to fifty-five." Walter Mitty drove on toward Waterbury in silence, the roaring of the SN202 through the worst storm in twenty years of Navy flying fading in the remote, intimate airways of his mind. "You're tensed up again," said Mrs. Mitty. "It's one of your days. I wish you'd let Dr. Renshaw look you over."

Walter Mitty stopped the car in front of the building where his wife went to have her hair done. "Remember to get those overshoes while I'm having my hair done," she said. "I don't need overshoes," said Mitty. She put her mirror back into her bag. "We've been all through that," she said, getting out of the car. "You're not a young man any longer." He raced the engine a little. "Why don't you wear your gloves? Have you lost your gloves?" Walter Mitty reached in a pocket and brought out the gloves. He put them on, but after she had turned and gone into the building and he had driven on to a red light, he took them off again. "Pick it up brother!" snapped a cop as the light changed, and Mitty hastily pulled on his gloves and lurched ahead. He drove around the streets aimlessly for a time, and then he drove past the hospital on his way to the parking lot.

. . . "It's the millionaire banker, Wellington McMillan," said the pretty nurse. "Yes?" said Walter Mitty, removing his gloves slowly. "Who has the case?" "Dr. Renshaw and Dr. Benbow, but there are two specialists here, Dr. Remington from New York and Dr. Pritchard-Mitford from London. He flew over." A door opened down a long, cool corridor and Dr. Renshaw came out. He looked distraught and haggard. "Hello, Mitty," he said. "We're having the devil's own time with McMillan, the millionaire banker and close personal friend of Roosevelt. Obstreosis of the ductal tract. Tertiary. Wish you'd take a look at him." "Glad to," said Mitty.

In the operating room there were whispered introductions: "Dr. Remington, Dr. Mitty. Dr. Pritchard-Mitford, Dr. Mitty." "I've read your book on steptothricosis," said Pritchard-Mitford, shaking hands. "A brilliant performance, sir." "Thank you," said Walter Mitty. "Didn't know you were in the States, Mitty," grumbled Remington. "Coals to Newcastle, bringing Mitford and me up here for a tertiary." "You are very kind," said Mitty. A huge, complicated machine, connected to the operating table, with many tubes and wires, began at this moment to go pocketa-pocketa-pocketa. "The new anaesthetizer is giving away!" shouted an interne. "There is no one in the East who knows how to

fix it!" "Quiet, man!" said Mitty, in a low, cool voice. He sprang to the machine, which was now going pocketa-pocketa-queep-pocketa-queep. He began fingering delicately a row of glistening dials. "Give me a fountain pen!" he snapped. Someone handed him a fountain pen. He pulled a faulty piston out of the machine and inserted the pen in its place. "That will hold for ten minutes," he said. "Get on with the operation." A nurse hurried over and whispered to Renshaw, and Mitty saw the man turn pale. "Coreopsis has set in," said Renshaw nervously. "If you would take over, Mitty?" Mitty looked at him and at the craven figure of Benbow, who drank, and at the grave, uncertain faces of the two great specialists. "If you wish," he said. They slipped a white gown on him; he adjusted a mask and drew on thin gloves; nurses handed him shining . . .

"Back it up, Mac! Look out for that Buick!" Walter Mitty jammed on the brakes. "Wrong lane, Mac," said the parking-lot attendant, looking at Mitty closely. "Gee. Yeh," muttered Mitty. He began cautiously to back out of the lane marked "Exit Only." "Leave her sit there," said the attendant. "I'll put her away." Mitty got out of the car. "Hey, better leave the key." "Oh," said Mitty, handing the man the ignition key. The attendant vaulted into the car, backed it up with insolent skill, and put it where it belonged.

They're so damn cocky, thought Walter Mitty, walking along Main Street; they think they know everything. Once he had tried to take his chains off, outside New Milford, and he had got them wound around the axles. A man had had to come out in a wrecking car and unwind them, a young, grinning garageman. Since then Mrs. Mitty always made him drive to a garage to have the chains taken off. The next time, he thought, I'll wear my right arm in a sling; they won't grin at me then. I'll have my right arm in a sling and they'll see I couldn't possibly take the chains off myself. He kicked at the slush on the sidewalk. "Overshoes," he said to himself, and he began looking for a shoe store.

When he came out into the street again, with the overshoes in a box under his arm, Walter Mitty began to wonder what the other thing was his wife had told him to get. She had told him, twice before they set out from their house for Waterbury. In a way he hated these weekly trips to town—he was always getting something wrong. Kleenex, he thought, Squibb's, razor blades? No. Toothpaste, toothbrush, bicarbonate, carborundum, initiative and referendum? He gave it up. But she would remember it. "Where's that what's-its-name?" she would ask. "Don't tell me you forgot that what's-its-name." A newsboy went by shouting something about the Waterbury trial.

. . . "Perhaps this will refresh your memory." The District Attorney suddenly thrust a heavy automatic at the quiet figure on the witness stand. "Have you ever seen this before?" Walter Mitty took the gun and examined it expertly. "This is my Webley-Vickers 50.80," he said calmly. An excited buzz ran around the courtroom. The Judge rapped for order. "You are a crack shot with any sort of firearms, I believe?" said the District Attorney, insinuatingly. "Objection!" shouted Mitty's attorney. "We have shown that the defendant could not have fired the shot. We have shown that he wore his right arm in a sling on the night of the fourteenth of July." Walter Mitty raised his hand briefly and the bickering attorneys were stilled. "With any known make of gun," he said evenly, "I could have killed Gregory Fitzhurst at three hundred feet *with my left hand*." Pandemonium broke loose in the courtroom. A woman's scream rose above the bedlam and suddenly a lovely, dark-haired girl was in Walter Mitty's arms. The District Attorney struck at her savagely. Without rising from his chair, Mitty let the man have it on the point of the chin. "You miserable cur!" ...

"Puppy biscuit," said Walter Mitty. He stopped walking and the buildings of Waterbury rose up out of the misty courtroom and surrounded him again. A woman who was passing laughed. "He said 'Puppy biscuit'," she said to her companion. "That man said 'Puppy biscuit' to himself." Walter Mitty hurried on. He went into an A. & P., not the first one he came to but a smaller one farther up the street. "I want some biscuit for small, young dogs," he said to the clerk. "Any special brand, sir?" The greatest pistol shot in the world thought a moment. "It says 'Puppies Bark for It' on the box," said Walter Mitty.

His wife would be through at the hairdresser's in fifteen minutes, Mitty saw in looking at his watch, unless they had trouble drying it; sometimes they had trouble drying it. She didn't like to get to the hotel first; she would want him to be there waiting for her as usual. He found a big leather chair in the lobby, facing a window, and he put the overshoes and the puppy biscuit on the floor beside it. He picked up an old copy of *Liberty* and sank down into the chair. "Can Germany Conquer the World Through the Air?" Walter Mitty looked at the pictures of bombing planes and of ruined streets.

... "The cannonading has got the wind up in young Raleigh, sir," said the sergeant. Captain Mitty looked up at him through tousled hair. "Get him to bed," he said wearily, "with the others. I'll fly alone." "But you can't, sir," said the sergeant anxiously. "It takes two men to handle that bomber and the Archies are pounding hell out of the air. Von Richtman's circus is between here and Saulier." "Somebody's got to get that ammunition

dump," said Mitty. "I'm going over. Spot of brandy?" He poured
a drink for the sergeant and one for himself. War thundered and
whined around the dugout and battered at the door. There was a
rending of wood and splinters flew through the room. "A bit of a
near thing," said Captain Mitty carelessly. "The box barrage is
closing in," said the sergeant. "We only live once, Sergeant," said
Mitty, with his faint, fleeting smile. "Or do we?" He poured
another brandy and tossed it off. "I never see a man could hold his
brandy like you, sir," said the sergeant. "Begging your pardon,
sir." Captain Mitty stood up and strapped on his huge Webley-
Vickers automatic. "It's forty kilometres through hell, sir," said
the sergeant. Mitty finished one last brandy. "After all," he said
softly, "what isn't?" The pounding of the cannon increased; there
was the rat-tat-tatting of machine guns, and from somewhere
came the menacing pocketa-pocketa-pocketa of the new flame-
throwers. Walter Mitty walked to the door of the dugout humming
"Auprès de Ma Blonde." He turned and waved to the sergeant.
"Cheerio!" he said....

86

Something struck his shoulder. "I've been looking all over this hotel for you," said Mrs. Mitty. "Why do you have to hide in this old chair? How did you expect me to find you?" "Things close in," said Walter Mitty vaguely. "What?" Mrs. Mitty said. "Did you get the what's-its-name? The puppy biscuit? What's in that box?" "Overshoes," said Mitty. "Couldn't you have put them on in the store?" "I was thinking," said Walter Mitty. "Does it ever occur to you that I am sometimes thinking?" She looked at him. "I'm going to take your temperature when I get you home," she said.

They went out through the revolving doors that made a faintly derisive whistling sound when you pushed them. It was two blocks to the parking lot. At the drugstore on the corner she said, "Wait here for me. I forgot something. I won't be a minute." She was more than a minute. Walter Mitty lighted a cigarette. It began to rain, rain with sleet in it. He stood up against the wall of the drugstore, smoking. . . He put his shoulders back and his heels together. "To hell with the handkerchief," said Walter Mitty scornfully. He took one last drag on his cigarette and snapped it away. Then, with that faint, fleeting smile playing about his lips, he faced the firing squad; erect and motionless, proud and disdainful, Walter Mitty the Undefeated, inscrutable to the last.

René Guillot

René Guillot (pronounced Ruhnay Gheeyo) was born in 1900 in France. In 1923 he went to French West Africa as a schoolteacher and made his home there for the next twenty-five years. During this time he gained a deep knowledge of the jungle and native life in the territory. He went hunting in the deepest parts of the jungle, travelled up the River Niger in a small boat, listened to the legends of the natives and studied the beliefs and customs of African tribes.

He did not begin using this knowledge in stories for young readers, however, until 1948, when *The White Shadow* was published. This tale of a French girl in Africa who makes friends with an African child was followed by a quartet of memorable animal stories: *Sama,* about a baby elephant; *Sirga,* the adventures of an African child and a lion cub; *Oworo,* a chimpanzee; and *Kpo the Leopard.* If you enjoy stories about the animal and human inhabitants of the jungle, or tales of high adventure, such as *Companions of Fortune,* which is about buccaneers on the high seas, there are over twenty books by René Guillot from which you can choose.

Running throughout his stories, which have often been compared to those of Rudyard Kipling (see *SHORT STORIES ONE*), is the theme of friendship. It may be friendship between white and coloured men, between animals, or, as in THE LION CUBS, between humans and animals.

During the Second World War René Guillot served in France and Germany, for which he was awarded the Croix de Guerre and other decorations. He finally returned to France in 1950 and retired from teaching ten years later. He died in 1969.

The Lion Cubs

by René Guillot

When they brought Marlow two little cubs, orphans of the bush, he hunted through his toolbox and all the odds and ends littering the mill room of the old sukala to try to find a feeding-bottle and some rubber teats.

"You see," he said to me, "I had last used one nearly a year back. That was for an antelope which I had not been able to save anyway."

In the end he had found the teats, slightly mildewed. He had them thoroughly boiled. Then he set about preparing lunch for these two poor little cubs who were making angry faces and growling with temper like tiger-cats.

"But what beautiful silky coats they had!" Marlow said. "Like thick, fluffy balls of plush. You know what I mean: it's stiff as well as silky."

The cubs refused to touch cow's milk. Then Marlow got hold of a goat, and Sammy milked it but the wild babies only spat at it—*psh!*—like infuriated cats.

"I wasn't going to give up for a little setback like that," said Marlow. "All the animals on my land were helpful—those who had milk, I mean, of course. Elephant's milk was the only kind I was not able to try. And I thought I was sure to be successful with my two awkward grumblers when I fed them warmed milk from one of my two giraffes—the smaller one. She had just given birth to a baby who's going on for twelve foot now.

"The cubs didn't even deign to wet their tongues in the giraffe's milk. Sammy drank it instead," said Marlow. "Actually that put

89

me wise to him. Sammy was a greedy chap. My baby giraffe was not thriving, and now I knew why. My boy was making himself nice cups of creamy coffee with what he stole from the giraffe's young one."

Marlow had called in Samoo.

"Samoo," he said, pointing to the cubs, "there's the latest present from the bush."

"You are the animals' friend," said Samoo.

"But there's nothing I can do for them."

"The bush does well what she does," replied the old Lobi.

Samoo, who was not far off a hundred years old, knew that in the Lobi country nature, things, trees, flowers, plants, skies, slow or treacherous waters, everything that exists between earth and heaven, in short, the bush, is capricious, self-willed, obstinate.

Samoo had learned not to cross her.

If Marlow wanted to try his strength against the age-old bush and go against her wishes he was free to do so.

"Yes," Marlow agreed, "she does well what she does. And so I am wondering, since she has sent me these two lion cubs, how she wants me to go about the job of preventing them dying of hunger."

He looked pensive for a moment. What he was about to propose to Samoo, the sorcerer of Laruna, was out of the ordinary. He must not put the old man off. The best thing would be if he could lead him to believe that he, Samoo, had made this staggering suggestion!

"Samoo," said Marlow, "these little savages are motherless."

"That is the truth."

"The bush does not wish this, Samoo."

"You say so," mumbled Samoo.

"And you agree with me. The bush does not want more motherless children than there are childless mothers."

The old sorcerer raised his head and pulled down the narrow peak of his leather cap over his forehead.

"Samoo," went on Marlow in an even tone, "the bush reigns everywhere, inside and outside, in the sukalas and on their flat terrace roofs ... everywhere."

"That is true," said Samoo.

"At Laruna, we have twice five roofs, five and five."

Marlow opened and closed his hand twice. The old man was listening.

"On one of those roofs I know that Yao sits."

"You know everything," replied the sorcerer.

"But could you tell me, Samoo, why that girl, who is called Yao, does not follow the women's custom? Tell me, do you know why? You are the chief elder of Laruna. You know the custom. The women do not usually stay on the terrace roof lamenting. They always go and lie at the end of the millet fields where the forest begins. But here is Yao staying on the roof of her sukala to cry."

The old sorcerer nodded his head. Obviously Great Man Marlow was turning his idea over in his head and not just once but many times, before it could be guessed. You had to be patient till the man explained himself.

Marlow said, "I know why Yao goes up on to the roof of her house. It is to mourn for her baby who died."

"Yes."

"It is also because from a roof one can see a long way into the distance. You can see what's coming. Do you understand, Samoo? If the bush wants to return Yao's son to her—the little boy who got lost in the forest—then..."

"Then Yao will be the first to see him come back," said the old man. "But you know perfectly well that the forest devoured her child."

"Did you see it devour him, Samoo?"

"No."

"Have you seen any bones?"

"No."

"Well then, why do you say that the forest devoured the boy? Let Yao wait until the bush gives her a sign. Perhaps her child will be returned to her."

A long silence. The old man was beginning to guess what the Great Man of Laruna was driving at.

"Samoo, you said a moment ago the bush does not want more motherless children than childless mothers. Look at these baby lions. They are kings of the savanna and all the woods as far as the Comoe and beyond."

The old man stood up. He bowed ceremoniously; then on the steps of the veranda he said:

"This evening, I'll send the girl to you."

And that same evening Yao came; she from whom the forest had stolen her child presented herself at Laruna. Her two brothers, trackers of Marlow's, came with her but stayed outside, sitting with their backs to the wall and their bows between their knees.

Sammy explained to the young woman what was expected of her at Laruna.

"I had to save those two little wild animals," said Marlow. "I did not know whether they would like this milk any better than the others, but I had to try it.

"The girl was very frightened. And I can understand her feelings. For a woman, a Lobi, to give the breast to the young of a lioness. . . .

"But if you'd seen those two little cubs after their first feed! They made such a fuss of their foster-mother. In three days the woman was touched with tenderness for her voracious babies. She fondled them, and washed and combed them, here at Laruna. I wasn't letting her go back home with those cubs to manage all on her own. No fear.

"For all that, the Lobi girl had not forgotten her child who had disappeared in the forest. Thinking of him she would sing simple little songs like those the women of the woods sing. And on her lap the two little cubs would be rolled up in a ball purring.

> My little one . . . my little one
> My little one.
> There is the sky
> My little one,
> There is the wood
> My little one,
> There is the day,
> There is the night,
> There are the big animals,
> My little one . . . my little one.

"And when she was quite used to feeding the cubs and rocking them in her lap and hearing them purr when they were full of milk, she altered her song a little, hardly anything really, but because there were two of them she sang:

> My little ones . . . my little ones
> My little ones.
> There is the sky . . .

"That was to go on for more than a month," said Marlow.

"The greedy little things loved their foster-mother, but the young of wild animals are not difficult to deceive. And then, they were growing visibly. A month-old cub is quite a size, and his woolly coat grows stiffer and begins to resemble the lordly lion's.

"One day I tried my cubs with a big bottleful of warm, sweetened cow's milk. They hesitated at first, then delightedly drank the lot. I thought that the young woman would now be glad to be with her own people again in her own home, and I sent her back to the village."

But the next day Marlow looked out, and there she was again with her tiny black plaits, her glass necklace, a blue bead in her nostril, coming up the hill to Laruna.

At the Bambassu she had stopped to pick some water flowers to give Marlow. She stroked her two children and sang them a song. She was lost without them.

"Had she gone up on to her house-roof when she got home to see whether the bush would give her a sign? Did she still hope her little boy might return?"

"I wonder," said Marlow. "I've no idea. But with Sammy's help as interpreter I promised the girl that I would speak to the bush. Perhaps she thought, in spite of her naïveté, that this was just one of those promises that one does not keep. However that may be, she came up regularly every day to see her babies, who now played with her outside. They would run races, and have a real rough and tumble. The cubs were strong and would push the girl over, but she would go off into peals of laughter and scramble up again."

"What became of the cubs?" I asked.

"I gave them back to the bush," Marlow said, "as soon as they began to gnaw bones. They were never given meat in my house. The first they ate was an antelope that I shot for them over by Dankana where I had taken them in the truck. I left them there beside the game. I'm satisfied that they soon got to know the savanna, and the region of the river. And the next day they killed their own meat for themselves."

"And the girl with the blue bead . . .?"

"She came to Laruna and found her children gone. I explained to her that the bush had taken them back and might perhaps return her own child to her in exchange."

It was six months since she had lost him. She had not forgotten him certainly. But now she had to face the further loss of her twins.

The Lobi women when they mourn do not shed tears.

"But she cried," said Marlow.

Then she went back to her village. She never came up to Marlow's house again now that the lion cubs were gone.

Marlow sent for Samoo.

"Samoo, how old was Yao's little boy?"

The old man reckoned it up. Marlow gathered that he would have been about a year old now.

"Was he beautiful?"

"He was beautiful," said Samoo.

"He had a birthmark on his arm, hadn't he?" said Marlow.

"No, on his forehead. A bluish mark like a cross."

"That's right. Samoo, send Yan the tracker to me tomorrow."

"Yan shall come to you tomorrow."

"He knows the language of the lions."

"Yes, Yan speaks with the lions."

And here is what the Great Man of Laruna devised, for he thought that the wise old bush wanted neither childless mothers nor motherless children.

He went round the distant villages. One finds orphans in the sukalas sometimes. He was looking for a baby a year old. The one he brought back secretly to Togbiéto did not have a birthmark on its forehead.

Marlow went to see the doctor and explained what he wanted. It could not be a very difficult matter to mark this baby boy of twelve months or just over with a blue cross on his forehead. A slight tattooing.

"Come back and fetch him in a week," said the doctor.

And Yan, the tracker who could talk with lions, had been summoned a second time to Marlow's house. He was a strapping fellow in the prime of life who went hunting weighed down with *gris-gris* round his wrists, neck, and ankles.

When it came to the attack he would approach any animal, no matter what, with his two-edged spear. His other hand was

clenched tightly upon all the courage and supernatural strength
that an elephant's tail complete with tuft could give him. Yan
never took his *mukala* (an old gun), except when he was hunting
elephant.

"I led him to a clearing opposite a little wood," said Marlow, "I
knew that lions were on the prowl. I told him to listen. He had an
extraordinarily keen ear. He listened a moment, then said, 'A lion.'

"I waited a while. The lion spoke again. Then I said to Yan,
'What does the animal want?' 'Me not know.' That was all I
needed. 'I know, Yan, what he wants.'

"And I explained to him that the lion was there to speak to him
on behalf of the bush. The wise old bush had something to
communicate to the village. But what—?

"Yan was thoughtful. These simple people can be touched by
anything supernatural."

Yan and Marlow remained a little longer listening to the lion in
the distance. At last the Great Man of Laruna said:

"Let's go."

As neither of them had understood, there was nothing they
could do but turn back home. Yan was troubled; he had not
understood the animal's message.

"Then,' said Marlow, "I drew him towards the wood. I knew very well what I was going to find there asleep on the grass: the little boy whom the doctor had marked with a bluish cross so that his mother might know him."

Yan gave a cry of surprise.

"A child . . ."

"Where?" Marlow said, feigning astonishment.

"There."

"So there is."

Then Marlow the sorcerer took the Lobi hunter by the shoulders.

"That's what the lion wanted to tell us," he said. "He was saying that the bush wants to give Yao back her child."

"Yao . . ." echoed Yan, full of wonder.

From her sukala roof Yao, if she was still watching the forest side, could see Yan, the hunter who spoke with the lions, coming back with a child in his arms. The lions had entrusted to him the precious burden.

And the woman recognized the blue mark.

In her heart she must have thanked her two foster-children who, now that they were lords of the forest, had not forgotten the woman who had suckled them.

And now that she had only one child again, the girl with the black plaits and the blue bead in her nostril began her song once more:

> My little one . . . my little one
> My little one.
> There is the sky
> My little one,
> There is the wood
> My little one,
> There is the day,
> There is the night,
> There is the lion . . .

Mark Twain

Mark Twain was born in 1835 in Florida, Missouri. His father died when he was twelve and he became a printer's apprentice for two local newspapers, to which he later contributed articles. Subsequently, he travelled through many parts of the USA working as a journeyman printer (see JOURNALISM IN TENNESSEE for a humorous account of small-town newspaper production). In 1857 he became a river pilot on the Mississippi steam boats but returned to journalism four years later. By 1865 he had gained a reputation as a leading humorist.

In 1876 came the first of his books for young people, *The Adventures of Tom Sawyer*, telling of a boy's escapades in a small town on the banks of the Mississippi. It was an immediate success and a hundred years later still remains one of the most popular boys' stories ever published. *The Adventures of Huckleberry Finn* had a similar reception and is also counted as one of the most widely read novels of all time. It deals with the adventures of Huck Finn, one of the leading characters in *Tom Sawyer*, when he runs away from his brutal father and, with an escaped Negro slave, Jim, travels down the Mississippi on a raft. Two sequels to the original *Tom Sawyer—Tom Sawyer Abroad* and *Tom Sawyer: Detective*—appeared in 1894 and 1896 respectively. Another book often enjoyed by young readers is *The Prince and the Pauper,* in which the Prince of England and a beggar boy change places.

Mark Twain was a pen name, derived from a call, signifying two fathoms, given by Mississippi river pilots when taking soundings. The author's real name was Samuel Clemens. He died in 1910.

Journalism in Tennessee

by Mark Twain

The editor of the Memphis *Avalanche* swoops thus mildly down upon a correspondent who posted him as a Radical:— "While he was writing the first word, the middle, dotting his i's, crossing his t's, and punching his period, he knew he was concocting a sentence that was saturated with infamy and reeking with falsehood."—*Exchange.*

I was told by the physician that a Southern climate would improve my health, and so I went down to Tennessee, and got a berth on the *Morning Glory and Johnson County War-Whoop* as associate editor. When I went on duty I found the chief editor sitting tilted back in a three-legged chair with his feet on a pine table. There was another pine table in the room and another afflicted chair, and both were half buried under newspapers and scraps and sheets of manuscript. There was a wooden box of sand, sprinkled with cigar stubs and "old soldiers," and a stove with a door hanging by its upper hinge. The chief editor had a long-tailed black frock-coat on, and white linen pants. His boots were small and neatly blacked. He wore a ruffled shirt, a large seal-ring, a standing collar of obsolete pattern, and a checkered neckerchief with the ends hanging down. Date of costume about 1848. He was smoking a cigar, and trying to think of a word, and in pawing his hair he had rumpled his locks a good deal. He was scowling fearfully, and I judged that he was concocting a particularly knotty editorial. He told me to take the exchanges and skim through them and write up the "Spirit of the Tennessee Press," condensing into the article all of their contents that seemed of interest.

I wrote as follows:

SPIRIT OF THE TENNESSEE PRESS

The editors of the *Semi-Weekly Earthquake* evidently labor under a misapprehension with regard to the Ballyhack railroad. It is not the object of the company to leave Buzzardville off to one side. On the contrary, they consider it one of the most important points along the line, and consequently can have no desire to slight it. The gentlemen of the *Earthquake* will, of course, take pleasure in making the correction.

John W. Blossom, Esq., the able editor of the Higginsville *Thunderbolt and Battle Cry of Freedom,* arrived in the city yesterday. He is stopping at the Van Buren House.

We observe that our contemporary of the Mud Springs *Morning Howl* has fallen into the error of supposing that the election of Van Werter is not an established fact, but he will have discovered his mistake before this reminder reaches him, no doubt. He was doubtless misled by incomplete election returns.

It is pleasant to note that the city of Blathersville is endeavoring to contract with some New York gentlemen to pave its well-nigh impassable streets with the Nicholson pavement. The *Daily Hurrah* urges the measure with ability, and seems confident of ultimate success.

I passed my manuscript over to the chief editor for acceptance, alteration, or destruction. He glanced at it and his face clouded. He ran his eye down the pages, and his countenance grew portentous. It was easy to see that something was wrong. Presently he sprang up and said:

"Thunder and lightning! Do you suppose I am going to speak of those cattle that way? Do you suppose my subscribers are going to stand such gruel as that? Give me the pen!"

I never saw a pen scrape and scratch its way so viciously, or plow through another man's verbs and adjectives so relentlessly. While he was in the midst of his work, somebody shot at him through the open window, and marred the symmetry of my ear.

"Ah," said he, "that is that scoundrel Smith, of the *Moral Volcano*—he was due yesterday." And he snatched a navy revolver from his belt and fired. Smith dropped, shot in the thigh. The shot spoiled Smith's aim, who was just taking a second chance, and he crippled a stranger. It was me. Merely a finger shot off.

Then the chief editor went on with his erasures and interlineations. Just as he finished them a hand-grenade came

down the stovepipe, and the explosion shivered the stove into a thousand fragments. However, it did no further damage, except that a vagrant piece knocked a couple of my teeth out.

"That stove is utterly ruined," said the chief editor.

I said I believed it was.

"Well, no matter—don't want it this kind of weather. I know the man that did it. I'll get him. Now, *here* is the way this stuff ought to be written."

I took the manuscript. It was scarred with erasures and interlineations till its mother wouldn't have known it if it had one. It now read as follows:

SPIRIT OF THE TENNESSEE PRESS

The inveterate liars of the *Semi-Weekly Earthquake* are evidently endeavoring to palm off upon a noble and chivalrous people another of their vile and brutal falsehoods with regard to that most glorious conception of the nineteenth century, the Ballyhack railroad. The idea that Buzzardville was to be left off at one side originated in their own fulsome brains—or rather in the settlings which *they* regard as brains. They had better swallow this lie if they want to save their abandoned reptile carcasses the cowhiding they so richly deserve.

That ass, Blossom, of the Higginsville *Thunderbolt and Battle Cry of Freedom,* is down here again sponging at the Van Buren.

We observe that the besotted blackguard of the Mud Springs *Morning Howl* is giving out, with his usual propensity for lying, that Van Werter is not elected. The heaven-born mission of journalism is to disseminate truth; to eradicate error; to educate, refine, and elevate the tone of public morals and manners, and make all men more gentle, more virtuous, more charitable, and in all ways better, and holier, and happier; and yet this black-hearted scoundrel degrades his great office persistently to the dissemination of falsehood, calumny, vituperation, and vulgarity.

Blathersville wants a Nicholson pavement—it wants a jail and a poorhouse more. The idea of a pavement in a one-horse town composed of two gin-mills, a blacksmith shop, and that mustard-plaster of a newspaper, the *Daily Hurrah!* The crawling insect, Buckner, who edits the *Hurrah,* is braying about his business with his customary imbecility, and imagining that he is talking sense.

"Now *that* is the way to write—peppery and to the point. Mush-and-milk journalism gives me the fan-tods."

About this time a brick came through the window with a splintering crash, and gave me a considerable jolt in the back. I moved out of range—I began to feel in the way.

The chief said, "That was the Colonel, likely. I've been expecting him for two days. He will be up now right away."

He was correct. The Colonel appeared in the door a moment afterward with a dragoon revolver in his hand.

He said, "Sir, have I the honor of addressing the poltroon who edits this mangy sheet?"

"You have. Be seated, sir. Be careful of the chair, one of its legs is gone. I believe I have the honor of addressing the putrid liar, Colonel Blatherskite Tecumseh?"

"Right, sir, I have a little account to settle with you. If you are at leisure we will begin."

"I have an article on the 'Encouraging Progress of Moral and Intellectual Development in America' to finish, but there is no hurry. Begin."

Both pistols rang out their fierce clamor at the same instant. The chief lost a lock of his hair, and the Colonel's bullet ended its career in the fleshy part of my thigh. The Colonel's left shoulder was clipped a little. They fired again. Both missed their men this time, but I got my share, a shot in the arm. At the third fire both gentlemen were wounded slightly, and I had a knuckle chipped. I then said, I believed I would go out and take a walk, as this was a private matter, and I had a delicacy about participating in it further. But both gentlemen begged me to keep my seat, and assured me that I was not in the way.

They then talked about the elections and the crops while they reloaded, and I fell to tying up my wounds. But presently they opened fire again with animation, and every shot took effect—but it is proper to remark that five out of the six fell to my share. The sixth one mortally wounded the Colonel, who remarked, with fine humor, that he would have to say good morning now, as he had business uptown. He then inquired the way to the undertaker's and left.

The chief turned to me and said, "I am expecting company to dinner, and shall have to get ready. It will be a favor to me if you will read proof and attend to the customers."

I winced a little at the idea of attending to the customers, but I was too bewildered by the fusillade that was still ringing in my ears to think of anything to say.

He continued, "Jones will be here at three—cowhide him. Gillespie will call earlier, perhaps—throw him out of the window. Ferguson will be along about four—kill him. That is all for today, I believe. If you have any odd time, you may write a blistering article on the police—give the chief inspector rats. The cowhides are under the table; weapons in the drawer—ammunition there in the corner—lint and bandages up there in the pigeonholes. In case of accident, go to Lancet, the surgeon, downstairs. He advertises—we take it out in trade."

He was gone. I shuddered. At the end of the next three hours I had been through perils so awful that all peace of mind and all cheerfulness were gone from me. Gillespie had called and thrown *me* out of the window. Jones arrived promptly, and when I got ready to do the cowhiding he took the job off my hands. In an encounter with a stranger, not in the bill of fare, I had lost my scalp. Another stranger, by the name of Thompson, left me a mere wreck and ruin of chaotic rags. And at last, at bay in the corner, and beset by an infuriated mob of editors, blacklegs, politicians,

and desperadoes, who raved and swore and flourished their weapons about my head till the air shimmered with glancing flashes of steel, I was in the act of resigning my berth on the paper when the chief arrived, and with him a rabble of charmed and enthusiastic friends. Then ensued a scene of riot and carnage such as no human pen, or steel one either, could describe. People were shot, probed, dismembered, blown up, thrown out of the window. There was a brief tornado of murky blasphemy, with a confused and frantic war-dance glimmering through it, and then all was over. In five minutes there was silence, and the gory chief and I sat alone and surveyed the sanguinary ruin that strewed the floor around us.

He said, "You'll like this place when you get used to it."

I said, "I'll have to get you to excuse me; I think maybe I might write to suit you after a while; as soon as I have had some practice and learned the language I am confident I could. But, to speak the plain truth, that sort of energy of expression has its inconveniences, and a man is liable to interruption. You see that yourself. Vigorous writing is calculated to elevate the public, no doubt, but then I do not like to attract so much attention as it calls forth. I can't write with comfort when I am interrupted so much as I have been today. I like this berth well enough, but I don't like to be left here to wait on the customers. The experiences are novel, I grant you, and entertaining, too, after a fashion, but they are not judiciously distributed. A gentleman shoots at you through the window and cripples *me*; a bombshell comes down the stove-pipe for your gratification and sends the stove door down *my* throat; a friend drops in to swap compliments with you, and freckles *me* with bullet-holes till my skin won't hold my principles; you go to dinner, and Jones comes with his cowhide, Gillespie throws me out of the window, Thompson tears all my clothes off, and an entire stranger takes my scalp with the easy freedom of an old acquaintance; and in less than five minutes all the blackguards in the country arrive in their war-paint, and proceed to scare the rest of me to death with their tomahawks. Take it altogether, I never had such a spirited time in all my life as I have had today. No; I like you, and I like your calm unruffled way of explaining things to the customers, but you see I am not used to it. The Southern heart is too impulsive; Southern hospitality is too lavish with the stranger. The paragraphs which I have written today, and into whose cold sentences your masterly hand has infused the fervent spirit of Tennessean journalism, will wake up another nest of hornets. All that mob of editors will come—and they will come hungry, too, and want somebody for breakfast. I shall have to bid you adieu. I decline to be present at these festivities. I came South for my health, I will go back on the same errand, and suddenly. Tennessean journalism is too stirring for me."

After which we parted with mutual regret, and I took apartments at the hospital.

Alan Garner

Alan Garner was born in 1935. He was educated at Alderley Edge Primary School, Manchester Grammar School and Oxford University. A keen athlete, he won a number of championships as a sprinter for Cheshire. He began writing towards the end of his service in the Royal Artillery. Today he still lives in Cheshire, in an old house called Toad Hall.

All his stories are concerned in some way with legends. But whereas GALGOID THE HEWER is set in early Ireland, all his novels are set in the modern world, into which he convincingly introduces the forces of ancient magic and myth. The first, *The Weirdstone of Brisingamen,* is about a magic stone which binds in sleep a band of knights until the day they must wake to fight Nastrond, the spirit of evil. But the wizard whose duty it is to guard the stone has lost it. Two children, Colin and Susan, discover the spell stone on Susan's bracelet, which is then seized by the evil powers. The children recover it and embark on an exciting chase through mines, woods and streams to return it to the wizard. In *The Moon of Gomrath,* Colin and Susan again become involved with Cadellin the wizard. This time Susan is placed in terrible danger and Colin can help her only by invoking The Old Magic, with terrifying consequences. *Elidor* also features Colin and Susan, but the setting is different—Manchester, instead of the hard, flat countryside around Alderley Edge.

Perhaps his most outstanding book is *The Owl Service,* in which three young people in a Welsh valley find themselves playing parts assigned to them by an old and dreadful myth. A vicious triangle reshapes itself as it has done again and again through the centuries. His latest novel is *Red Shift.*

Galgoid the Hewer

A Story for Christmas

by Alan Garner

There was a man living in Benbecula called Galgoid the Hewer: he was brother to Gilla Stagshank, the Chief Leaper of Ireland, and his was the most widespreading sword among the thirteen kings of the north.

Now it happened on a day of winter that Galgoid the Hewer and his men rode back from the valley of the five sons of Dorath, with the heads of the five sons of Dorath on their belts and their cattle before them. And they came at the mouth of dark and lateness to a hill above the shore, and there stood three ships filled with men. Their swords were white as lime, and their spears like death.

It was Morgor son of Limuris, from barren Caer Dathal, that had come. He was cousin to Galgoid on his mother's side, and green longing was in his heart for Benbecula. Galgoid rode down to the water, and spoke.

"Morgor son of Limuris, why are you come and the men of Caer Dathal in arms behind you?"

And Morgor said: "I am come for Benbecula of the Herds, which is mine through my mother, who had it from Gofynion the Old, who was grandmother to you and to me."

Galgoid answered him: "The white shield must be cloven, and cruel spear break on spear, ere I will share my inheritance. Is it a Rout or a Destruction, cousin?"

"A Destruction," said Morgor. "Since I, too, will not share my inheritance. In Benbecula widowhood awaits women."

Then the men of Benbecula gathered each a stone to make a

cairn. A pillar-stone they used to plant when there would be a Rout, a cairn for a Destruction. Everyone that would come safe out of the battle would take his stone from the cairn. The cairn on Benbecula is taller than the shadow of a man in the evening.

When this was done, Galgoid charged upon the ships. The first man he killed was Elestron, chief lord of Menevia. The iron bit through the cords of his neck, and the numbing death mists came upon him: his breath reddened the foam.

Then Galgoid rode on, his spear dark and dripping, and the battle glory in his eyes. He came to Osbrit Longhand, one of the Three Crowns of the Isle of Britain, whose axe was cutting helms like cloth and making many a son of Benbecula headless. Galgoid took him through the joints of his harness, and he laid his lips to the sand and there died. But as he fell, Osbrit broke the spear, pulling the haft with him beneath the water. Then Galgoid unsheathed his sword, whose name was Fragarach, which means Answerer: it was fated to kill a man each time it was drawn, and it was by this sword that Galgoid was called the Hewer.

Into the night and the full of the moon the battle rejoiced. Morgor son of Limuris brought his men to land, so that Galgoid and his men stood down from their horses, and Galgoid sprang across the rocks like a cloak on the back of a shadow, and with his arm made pools of blood: a long stream of light there was from his hand, and those whom he met were not met again.

The next man was Rofer Singlespit. He was so ugly that none had struck him: they thought he was a devil fighting. His sword had fed many a brown eagle, but Fragarach came down on his head, and the skull broke and the brains lay on the stones, and that was his death.

Then Galgoid the Hewer went as a flame of fire through the ranks of Morgor son of Limuris, and they fell before him sooner than broken rushes to the ground.

On a high rock stood Midhir Yellowmane, one of the Three Golden Herdsmen of Britain. He was from Inis Escandra, a magical country that lies to the northwards of the black watery isle, and his arm had given the iron death to thirty men that night. Galgoid the Hewer came to him, and they fought hatingly, without a word for each other: then Midhir's foot betrayed him of

108

the rock, and he fell, and he knew that never again in his living life of the world would he see cattle grow on the hill of Ben Hederin, nor wander home through the Pass of Murmuring.

But as Galgoid lifted his arm to send Midhir into darkness he saw a light stand out above the sea, a star of flame and ice, clear as the dew on Tara's mound, and his eyes were dazzled, so that the Answerer sang on the rock and did not taste the flesh of Midhir. The star was blueness and whiteness, beauty and terror, keener than Fragarach that would take alike iron and bronze and bone.

He lifted his arm again, but the light was in his eyes, and clouds of weakness came upon him, and he could not strike the blow. The light seemed to show him all the goodness in the man, all that he had won, and the richness of his destiny, the royal sons and daughters that would grow under his care. And Galgoid saw, too, his own joy of life, and he could not take that from another.

He turned from Midhir, thinking to cool Fragarach with baser blood, yet each time he came to the killing the star blinded him, and he saw only worth in the man and waste in his death, and there was no knowing under the white moon what to do, for the men of Caer Dathal were hard upon him when they saw his black trouble, his red difficulty, his grim plight. Yet even then Galgoid the Hewer

could not kill, though his death was in every sword. He thrust his shield before him and did not remember the horses, but stretched out on foot, fleeing. And a mist came blind and dark, so that no eye could see, and no man could discern.

"Keep with me!" cried Galgoid the Hewer to his kinsmen, and there answered him a hundred. The mist was so thick that he could not see his shield, and he cried again, and there answered him a score, and he cried out again, and there answered him but three; and next time he cried, none answered him at all. And then he came out above the mist, and all he saw in the heavens was the racing moon. Close by his feet sat the Nic-a-phi, the Sorrowful One of the Black Head, washing the bloody garments of those that were to die in battle. She was crooked, thatched with elf-locks, rough as heather.

"What brings you from the feast of arms, Galgoid son of Dela son of Loth?" she said.

"It is clouds of weakness that are on me. There was a star above the east, and the light of it has unmanned my sword."

"It is a sign to you," said the Nic-a-phi. "At this hour is come into the world that which makes blood a shame to the hands. No more is there joy in the cry of the sword."

"How shall it be?" said Galgoid the Hewer. "I have been accustomed to blood among the wrathful, a spear-thrust to the greed of Morgor. Shall all put off their armour and wait for straw-death in old age? Shall there be no strength to my arm, nor land to my name?"

"Alas for men," said the Sorrowful One of the Black Head. "Few will put off their armour; so you may not. But no more will you glory in war with the shining wing, though you must kill. But you shall kill in the knowing of each man's death, and the blood on your hands, and that only when justice is yours, as now. Ride no more as you rode against the five sons of Dorath, Galgoid son of Dela son of Loth."

Then a drowse of sleep and a load of slumber fell upon the man: when he woke it was day; near to him his mare Gwelugan cropped the turf. But the starlight was in him, and he thought to go away, leaving all behind, and to live his life in peace. And then he looked from the hillside on to the flying spears that tinged with blue the wings of the dawn, and Morgor son of Limuris fighting to make truth by blood, and Galgoid the Hewer turned his face that way, heavy in his heart, and rode down between the shafts and arrows of white iron to the shouting on the sea, to the lance-darting trembling of slaughter.

Henry Lawson

Henry Lawson was born in 1876 on the gold diggings near Grenfell in New South Wales. His father was a Norwegian sailor turned carpenter, his mother a strong-minded Australian with very definite views on democracy and the rights of women. At the age of fourteen he began work as a carpenter, the first of many jobs.

When his parents separated, he followed his mother to Sydney and began to write articles and poetry for newspapers and magazines, including one run by his mother. From her he inherited not only his desire to write but also his socialist views; during the shearers' strike in 1890 he wrote poems in support of the strikers. Always a solitary, unsettled man, he wandered about the thinly populated Australian outback in the depression years of the early 1890s, gaining many insights into the character of the Australian bushman.

He married in 1896 and went to live in Perth, where he wrote some of his best stories. But he was lonely and unhappy and after a few years made his way back to Sydney, as he also did at three later periods in his life—after working in a little Maori school in New Zealand, after three years as an author in London, and after a spell on a government farm in New South Wales. He died in 1922.

He wrote a large number of articles, poems and novels, but it is for his short stories that he is best remembered, particularly those in *When the Billy Boils, On the Track and Over the Sliprails* and *Joe Wilson and his Mates.* WAGGING IT and THE IRON-BARK CHIP are both good examples of his humour and his understanding of life in the Australian bush.

The Iron-Bark Chip

by Henry Lawson

Dave Regan and party—bush fencers, tank-sinkers, rough carpenters, etc.—were finishing the third and last culvert of their contract on the last section of the new railway line, and had already sent in their vouchers for the completed contract, so that there might be no excuse for extra delay in connection with the cheque.

Now it had been expressly stipulated in the plans and specifications that the timber for certain beams and girders was to be iron-bark and no other, and Government inspectors were authorised to order the removal from the ground of any timber or material they might deem inferior, or not in accordance with the stipulations. The railway contractor's foreman and inspector of sub-contractors was a practical man and a bushman, but he had been a timber-getter himself; his sympathies were bushy, and he was on winking terms with Dave Regan. Besides, extended time was expiring, and the contractors were in a hurry to complete the line. But the Government inspector was a reserved man who poked round on his independent own and appeared in lonely spots at unexpected times—with apparently no definite object in life—like a grey kangaroo bothered by a new wire fence, but unsuspicious of the presence of humans. He wore a grey suit, rode, or mostly led, an ashen-grey horse; the grass was long and grey, so he was seldom spotted until he was well within the horizon and bearing leisurely down on a party of sub-contractors, leading his horse.

Now iron-bark was scarce and distant on those ridges, and

another timber, similar in appearance, but much inferior in grain and "standing" quality, was plentiful and close at hand. Dave and party were "about full of" the job and place, and wanted to get their cheque and be gone to another "spec" they had in view. So they came to reckon they'd get the last girder from a handy tree, and have it squared, in place, and carefully and conscientiously tarred before the inspector happened along, if he did. But they didn't. They got it squared, and ready to be lifted into its place; the kindly darkness of tar was ready to cover a fraud that took four strong men with crow-bars and levers to shift; and now (such is the regular cussedness of things) as the fraudulent piece of timber lay its last hour on the ground, looking and smelling, to their guilty imaginations, like anything but iron-bark, they were aware of the Government inspector drifting down upon them obliquely, with something of the atmosphere of a casual Bill or Jim who had dropped out of his easy-going track to see how they were getting on, and borrow a match. They had more than half hoped that, as he had visited them pretty frequently during the progress of the work, and knew how near it was to completion, he wouldn't bother coming any more. But it's the way with the Government. You might move heaven and earth in vain endeavour to get the "Govermunt" to flutter an eyelash over something of the most momentous importance to yourself and mates and the district—even to the country; but just when you are leaving authority severely alone, and have strong reasons for not wanting to worry or interrupt it, and not desiring it to worry about you, it will take a fancy into its head to come along and bother.

"It's always the way!" muttered Dave to his mates. "I knew the beggar would turn up! . . . And the only cronk log we've had, too!" he added, in an injured tone. "If this had 'a' been the only blessed iron-bark in the whole contract, it would have been all right. . . . Good-day sir!" (to the inspector). "It's hot?"

The inspector nodded. He was not of an impulsive nature. He got down from his horse and looked at the girder in an abstracted way; and presently there came into his eyes a dreamy, far-away, sad sort of expression, as if there had been a very sad and painful occurrence in his family, way back in the past, and that piece of timber in some way reminded him of it and brought the old sorrow

home to him. He blinked three times, and asked, in a subdued tone:
"Is that iron-bark?"

Jack Bently, the fluent liar of the party, caught his breath with a jerk and coughed, to cover the gasp and gain time. "I—iron-bark? Of course it is! I thought you would know iron-bark, mister." (Mister was silent.) "What else d'yer think it is?"

The dreamy, abstracted expression was back. The inspector, by-the-way, didn't know much about timber, but he had a great deal of instinct, and went by it when in doubt.

"L—look here, mister!" put in Dave Regan, in a tone of innocent puzzlement and with a blank bucolic face. "B—but don't the plans and specifications say iron-bark? Ours does, anyway. I—I'll git the papers from the tent and show yer, if yer like."

It was not necessary. The inspector admitted the fact slowly. He stooped, and with an absent air picked up a chip. He looked at it abstractedly for a moment, blinked his threefold blink; then, seeming to recollect an appointment, he woke up suddenly and asked briskly:

"Did this chip come off that girder?"

Blank silence. The inspector blinked six times, divided in threes, rapidly, mounted his horse, said "Day", and rode off.

Regan and party stared at each other.

"Wha—what did he do that for?" asked Andy Page, the third in the party.

"Do what for, you fool?" enquired Dave.

"Ta—take that chip for?"

"He's taking it to the office!" snarled Jack Bently.

"What—what for? What does he want to do that for?"

"To get it blanky well analysed! You ass! Now are yer satisfied?" And Jack sat down hard on the timber, jerked out his pipe, and said to Dave, in a sharp, toothache tone:

"Gimmiamatch!"

"We—well! What are we to do now?" enquired Andy, who was the hardest grafter, but altogether helpless, hopeless, and useless in a crisis like this.

"Grain and varnish the bloomin' culvert!" snapped Bently.

But Dave's eyes, that had been ruefully following the inspector, suddenly dilated. The inspector had ridden a short distance along the line, dismounted, thrown the bridle over a post, laid the chip (which was too big to go in his pocket) on top in the direction of the fencing party, who had worked up on the other side, a little more than opposite the culvert.

Dave took in the lay of the country at a glance and thought rapidly.

"Gimme an iron-bark chip!" he said suddenly.

Bently, who was quick-witted when the track was shown him, as is a kangaroo dog (Jack ran by sight, not scent), glanced in the line of Dave's eyes, jumped up, and got a chip about the same size as that which the inspector had taken.

Now the "lay of the country" sloped generally to the line from both sides, and the angle between the inspector's horse, the fencing party, and the culvert was well within a clear concave space; but a couple of hundred yards back from the line and parallel to it (on the side on which Dave's party worked their timber) a fringe of scrub ran to within a few yards of a point which would be about in line with a single tree on the cleared slope, the horse, and the fencing party.

Dave took the iron-bark chip, ran along the bed of the watercourse into the scrub, raced up the siding behind the bushes, got safely, though without breathing, across the exposed space, and brought the tree into line between him and the inspector, who was talking to the fencers. Then he began to work quickly down the slope towards the tree (which was a thin one), keeping it in line, his arms close to his sides, and working, as it were, down the trunk of the tree, as if the fencing party were kangaroos and Dave was trying to get a shot at them. The inspector, by-the-bye, had a habit of glancing now and then in the direction of his horse, as though under the impression that it was flighty and restless and inclined to bolt on opportunity. It was an anxious moment for all parties concerned—except the inspector. They didn't want *him* to be perturbed. And, just as Dave reached the foot of the tree, the inspector finished what he had to say to the fencers, turned, and started to walk briskly back to his horse. There was a thunderstorm coming. Now was the critical moment—there were certain pre-arranged signals between Dave's party and the fencers which might have interested the inspector, but none to meet a case like this.

Jack Bently gasped, and started forward with an idea of intercepting the inspector and holding him for a few minutes in bogus conversation. Inspirations come to one at a critical moment, and it flashed on Jack's mind to send Andy instead. Andy looked as innocent and guileless as he was, but was uncomfortable in the vicinity of "funny business", and must have an honest excuse. "Not that that mattered," commented Jack afterwards; "it would have taken the inspector ten minutes to get at what Andy was driving at, whatever it was."

"Run, Andy! Tell him there's a heavy thunderstorm coming and he'd better stay in our humpy till it's over. Run! Don't stand staring like a blanky fool. He'll be gone!"

Andy started. But just then, as luck would have it, one of the fencers started after the inspector, hailing him as "Hi, mister!" He wanted to be set right about the survey or something—or to pretend to want to be set right—from motives of policy which I haven't time to explain here.

That fencer explained afterwards to Dave's party that he "seen what you coves was up to", and that's why he called the inspector back. But he told them that after they had told their yarn—which was a mistake.

"Come back, Andy!" cried Jack Bently.

Dave Regan slipped round the tree, down on his hands and knees, and made quick time through the grass which, luckily, grew pretty tall on the thirty or forty yards of slope between the tree and the horse. Close to the horse, a thought struck Dave that pulled him up, and sent a shiver along his spine and a hungry feeling under it. The horse would break away and bolt! But the case was desperate. Dave ventured an interrogatory "Cope, cope, cope?" The horse turned its head wearily and regarded him with a mild eye, as if he'd expected him to come, and come on all fours, and wondered what had kept him so long; then he went on thinking. Dave reached the foot of the post, the horse obligingly leaning over on the other leg. Dave reared head and shoulders cautiously behind the post, like a snake; his hand went up twice, swiftly—the first time he grabbed the inspector's chip, and the second time he put the iron-bark one in its place. He drew down and back, and scuttled off for the tree like a gigantic tailless goanna.

A few minutes later he walked up to the culvert from along the creek, smoking hard to settle his nerves.

The sky seemed to darken suddenly; the first great drops of the thunderstorm came pelting down. The inspector hurried to his horse, and cantered off along the line in the direction of the fettlers' camp.

He had forgotten all about the chip, and left it on top of the post!

Dave Regan sat down on the beam in the rain and swore comprehensively.

H. E. Bates

H. E. Bates was born in 1905. Educated at Kettering Grammar School, he worked as a clerk and as a reporter on a local paper before having his first book published at the age of twenty. Over the next fifteen years his novels mainly dealt with the grim realities of life and death in rural England.

During the Second World War he served as a Squadron Leader in the Royal Air Force and, under the pen name Flying Officer X, wrote several volumes of stories about airmen and life in the services. From 1942 to 1945 he was posted overseas and from what he saw of war against the Japanese in Burma and India sprang such novels as *The Jacaranda Tree* and *The Purple Plain*. Perhaps the most famous of his war stories is *Fair Stood the Wind for France*, about a British bomber crew forced down over France.

SILAS THE GOOD, which is taken from the collection *My Uncle Silas*, demonstrates a facet of his work which is sometimes overlooked—his ability to create comic characters and hilarious incidents. Uncle Silas is a cranky, crotchety little man, a poacher and a liar, with an unquenchable thirst for cowslip wine and an ever-open eye for the ladies. In the same vein are *The Darling Buds of May, A Breath of French Air* and *When the Green Woods Laugh*. For sheer entertainment this trilogy of books about the Larkin family is hard to beat. Pop ("Larkin by name, Larkin by nature"), Ma, munching crisps and shaking with laughter, their numerous and magnificently named offspring, and the newly recruited Mr. Charlton, provide great comedy.

Silas the Good

by H. E. Bates

In a life of ninety-five years, my Uncle Silas found time to try most things, and there was a time when he became a grave-digger.

The churchyard at Solbrook stands a long way outside the village on a little mound of bare land above the river valley.

And there, dressed in a blue shirt and mulatto brown corduroys and a belt that resembled more than anything a length of machine shafting, my Uncle Silas used to dig perhaps a grave a month.

He would work all day there at the blue-brown clay without seeing a soul, with no one for company except crows, the pewits crying over the valley or the robin picking the worms out of the thrown-up earth. Squat, misshapen, wickedly ugly, he looked something like a gargoyle that had dropped off the roof of the little church, something like a brown dwarf who had lived too long after his time and might go on living and digging the graves of others for ever.

He was digging a grave there once on the south side of the churchyard on a sweet, sultry day in May, the grass already long and deep, with strong golden cowslips rising everywhere among the mounds and the gravestones, and bluebells hanging like dark smoke under the creamy waterfalls of hawthorn bloom.

By noon he was fairly well down with the grave, and had fixed his boards to the sides. The spring had been very dry and cold, but now, in the shelter of the grave, in the strong sun, it seemed like midsummer. It was so good that Silas sat in the bottom of the grave and had his dinner, eating his bread and mutton off the thumb, and washing it down with the cold tea he always carried in

121

a beer-bottle. After eating, he began to feel drowsy, and finally he went to sleep there, at the bottom of the grave, with his wet, ugly mouth drooping open and the beer-bottle in one hand and resting on his knee.

He had been asleep for a quarter of an hour or twenty minutes when he woke up and saw someone standing at the top of the grave, looking down at him. At first he thought it was a woman. Then he saw his mistake. It was a female.

He was too stupefied and surprised to say anything, and the female stood looking down at him, very angry at something, poking holes in the grass with a large umbrella. She was very pale, updrawn and skinny, with a face, as Silas described it, like a turnip lantern with the candle out. She seemed to have size nine boots on and from under her thick black skirt Silas caught a glimpse of an amazing knickerbocker leg, baggy, brown in colour, and about the size of an airship.

He had not time to take another look before she was at him. She

waved her umbrella and cawed at him like a crow, attacking him for indolence and irreverence, blasphemy and ignorance.

She wagged her head and stamped one of her feet, and every time she did so the amazing brown bloomer seemed to slip a little farther down her leg, until Silas felt it would slip off altogether. Finally, she demanded, scraggy neck craning down at him, what did he mean by boozing down there, on holy ground, in a place that should be sacred for the dead?

Now at the best of times it was difficult for my Uncle Silas, with ripe, red lips, one eye bloodshot and bleary, and a nose like a crusty strawberry, not to look like a drunken sailor. But there was only one thing that he drank when he was working, and that was cold tea. It was true that it was always cold tea with whisky in it, but the basis remained, more or less, cold tea.

Silas let the female lecture him for almost five minutes, and then he raised his panama hat and said, "Good afternoon, ma'am. Ain't the cowslips out nice?"

"Not content with desecrating holy ground," she said, "you're intoxicated, too!"

"No, ma'am," he said, "I wish I was."

"Beer!" she said. "Couldn't you leave the beer alone in here, of all places?"

Silas held up the beer-bottle. "Ma'am," he said, "what's in here wouldn't harm a fly. It wouldn't harm you."

"It is responsible for the ruin of thousands of homes all over England!" she said.

"Cold tea," Silas said.

Giving a little sort of snort she stamped her foot and the bloomer-leg jerked down a little lower. "Cold tea!"

"Yes, ma'am. Cold tea." Silas unscrewed the bottle and held it up to her. "Go on, ma'am, try it. Try it if you don't believe me."

"Thank you. Not out of that bottle."

"All right. I got a cup," Silas said. He looked in his dinner basket and found an enamel cup. He filled it with tea and held it up to her. "Go on, ma'am, try it. Try it. It won't hurt you."

"Well!" she said, and she reached down for the cup. She took it and touched her thin bony lips to it. "Well, it's certainly some sort of tea."

"Just ordinary tea, ma'am," Silas said. "Made this morning. You ain't drinking it. Take a good drink."

She took a real drink then, washing it round her mouth.

"Refreshin', ain't it?" Silas said.

"Yes," she said, "it's very refreshing."

"Drink it up," he said. "Have a drop more. I bet you've walked a tidy step?"

"Yes," she said, "I'm afraid I have. All the way from Bedford. Rather farther than I thought. I'm not so young as I used to be."

"Pah!" Silas said. "Young? You look twenty." He took his coat and spread it on the new earth above the grave. "Sit down and rest yourself, ma'am. Sit down and look at the cowslips."

Rather to his surprise, she sat down. She took another drink of the tea and said, "I think I'll unpin my hat." She took off her hat and held it in her lap.

"Young?" Silas said. "Ma'am, you're just a chicken. Wait till you're as old as me and then you can begin to talk. I can remember the Crimea!"

"Indeed?" she said. "You must have had a full and varied life."

"Yes, ma'am."

She smiled thinly, for the first time. "I am sorry I spoke as I did. It upset me to think of anyone drinking in this place."

"That's all right, ma'am," Silas said. "That's all right. I ain't touched a drop for years. Used to, ma'am. Bin a regular sinner."

Old Silas reached up to her with the bottle and said, "Have some more, ma'am," and she held down the cup and filled it up again. "Thank you," she said. She looked quite pleasant now, softened by the tea and the smell of cowslips and the sun on her bare head. The bloomer-leg had disappeared and somehow she stopped looking like a female and became a woman.

"But you've reformed now?" she said.

"Yes, ma'am," Silas said, with a slight shake of his head, as though he were a man in genuine sorrow. "Yes, ma'am. I've reformed."

"It was a long fight?"

"A long fight, ma'am? I should say it was, ma'am. A devil of a long fight." He raised his panama hat a little. "Beg pardon, ma'am. That's another thing I'm fighting against. The language."

124

"And the drink," she said, "how far back does that go?"

"Well, ma'am," Silas said, settling back in the grave, where he had been sitting all that time, "I was born in the hungry 'forties. Bad times, ma'am, very bad times. We was fed on barley pap, ma'am, if you ever heard talk of barley pap. And the water was bad, too, ma'am. Very bad. Outbreaks of smallpox and typhoid and all that. So we had beer, ma'am. Everybody had beer. The babies had beer. So you see, ma'am," Silas said, "I've been fighting against it for eighty years and more. All my puff."

"And now you've conquered it?"

"Yes, ma'am," said my Uncle Silas, who had drunk more in eighty years than would keep a water-mill turning, "I've conquered it." He held up the beer-bottle. "Nothing but cold tea. You'll have some more cold tea, ma'am, won't you?"

"It's very kind of you," she said.

So Silas poured out another cup of the cold tea and she sat on the graveside and sipped it in the sunshine, becoming all the time more and more human.

"And no wonder," as Silas would say to me afterwards, "seeing it was still the winter ration we were drinking. You see, I had a summer ration with only a nip of whisky in it, and then I had a winter ration wi' pretty nigh a mugful in it. The weather had been cold up to that day and I hadn't bothered to knock the winter ration off."

They sat there for about another half an hour, drinking the cold tea, and during that time there was nothing she did not hear about my Uncle Silas's life: not only how he had reformed on the beer and was trying to reform on the language but how he had long since reformed on the ladies and the horses and the doubtful stories and the lying and everything else that a man can reform on.

Indeed, as he finally climbed up out of the grave to shake hands with her and say good afternoon, she must have got the impression that he was a kind of ascetic lay brother.

Except that her face was very flushed, she walked away with much the same dignity as she had come. There was only one thing that spoiled it. The amazing bloomer-leg had come down again, and Silas could not resist it.

"Excuse me, ma'am," he called after her, "but you're liable to

126

lose your knickerbockers."

She turned and gave a dignified smile and then a quick, saucy kind of hitch to her skirt, and the bloomer-leg went up, as Silas himself said, as sharp as a blind in a shop-window.

That was the last he ever saw of her. But that afternoon, on the 2.45 up-train out of Solbrook, there was a woman with a large umbrella in one hand and a bunch of cowslips in the other. In the warm, crowded carriage there was a smell of something stronger than cold tea, and it was clear to everyone that one of her garments was not in its proper place. She appeared to be a little excited, and to everybody's embarrassment she talked a great deal.

Her subject was someone she had met that afternoon.

"A good man," she told them. "A good man."